CROOK Q

CROOK Q

RED RAIN #2

RACHEL NEWHOUSE

rachelnewhouse.com

To David
whose unapologetic fanfiction
made this all possible

MAY 2076

1

I was graduating, and my teacher couldn't be more disappointed.

At most schools, graduating means you have succeeded. The virtual diploma signifies your achievement and grants you acceptance and opportunities in life. Teachers will do everything to ensure their students pass the final test.

For my class, however, graduating means we have failed. The virtual diploma demotes us to unteachable savages, and our teachers will do everything they can to ensure we drop out as soon as possible.

Today I graduate. Today I officially become a failure, an inmate who went through years of government schooling and still refused to sign the file. A Christian who survived hundreds of hours of conditioning, belittling, and propagandizing and still won't deny her religion.

Unassimilated. Reprobate. Criminal without any rights of citizenship.

Those were the terms my homeroom teacher hurled at me as he tried to dissuade me from accepting my diploma. It took all my willpower not to smile at him.

I was mildly surprised when he kept his tirade brief. I guess he finally understood that if I hadn't succumbed after being in his high school class for four years, another fifteen minutes of lecturing wouldn't make a difference.

"The principal will see you," he finished with a dismissive wave of his hand. He ungracefully flopped down in his chair and looked entirely fed-up, clearly wondering how all *his* years of schooling had condemned him to this moment.

I indulged in a cheeky smirk as I skipped out of the classroom and down the hall.

I composed myself as I came within sight of the principal's closed door. A pinch of fear wiped the smile off my face.

I desperately hoped the principal just wanted to talk to me. Sometimes being sent to the office meant someone else was here to see me—like Mrs. Nolan.

Banishing memories of the buttery voice from my head, I straightened my shoulders and rapped on the door.

"Come in, Philadelphia."

I offered up a quick prayer as I pushed the door open and stepped inside.

The principal was sitting with her hands folded on the desk, staring straight at me. I wondered how long she had been posed like that, waiting for my arrival.

"Decided to graduate, have you?" she declared.

She didn't sound as frustrated about it as my homeroom teacher—probably because she wasn't surprised.

"Yes, ma'am," I replied.

"Sit down."

I obeyed, and she shoved a tablet computer across the desk towards me. "You need to sign this file indicating that you have been offered remedial services through our institution and have voluntarily refused them." She tapped the legal document displayed on the screen. "You're acknowledging that, due to your unassimilated status at graduation, you will not be receiving a full high school diploma and are not entitled to the rights and privileges associated with one, although your academic record will still be posted to your file for future reference."

I thought it was delightfully ironic that I had to sign a file stating that I refused to sign the other file—the file that said I agreed to submit to United regulations as an assimilated citizen, which included denial of any and all religious, racial, and national identities. I suppose, since they couldn't get me to sign *that* file, they would get me to sign another, just for formality's sake.

I couldn't keep the smile off my face as I picked up the stylus and wrote my signature as tidily as possible.

The principal typed on her keyboard, and another legal document appeared on the tablet. "And this is your consent to be submitted for consideration in our Assisted Employment Program."

I squinted at the fine print on the document, waiting for her to explain before I signed.

"As an unassimilated citizen, you are eligible to be employed in select fields under the supervision of the United. Inclusion in the program also makes you eligible for opportunities for higher education and specialized training. Please note, however, that unassimilated citizens have far fewer opportunities for employment and education than citizens with full rights."

I looked up to find her gazing down her nose at me. I knew that was the final prod—one last opportunity to sign the file, join the Outside, and get a real job.

"No thank you, ma'am," I replied.

She didn't even blink. Turning back to her screen, she continued to recite: "If admitted, you will be assigned a job at the United's discretion. Your position and hours will be regulated by the government, and you will serve under the supervision of certified employers. You will not earn monetary compensation, but you may receive extra credit on your account for the purchase of necessary items, as deemed appropriate by the government based on your performance."

I went ahead and signed the file as she talked. I knew from experience that the employment program wasn't as horrible as she made it sound. Daddy had been working through the program since we had been contained, and he said it was like working a regular job, except that all your paychecks were in the form of credit to use through the United's approved catalog. But since the unassimilated could only own approved items anyway, that didn't seem like a huge sacrifice.

"Now, we need to fill out your application. Have you ever held any kind of job before?"

I set the stylus down and frowned at her. Didn't the United already have that information on file? They had been in complete control of my entire life for the past five years and had a pretty good hold on it before that; the government would know if I had ever held a job.

But I knew better than to answer sarcastically; Daddy said sarcasm wasn't respectful. "No, ma'am."

She nodded and clicked her mouse. "Have you had any special training for any particular fields?"

She ought to have known the answer to that, too—unassimilated citizens couldn't get any education except through the government. "No."

She clicked another box on the application. "And in what fields do your family members work?"

"My father and brother are scientists," I said, hoping she wouldn't ask me what branch of science. I could never keep them straight. "But I've never assisted them professionally," I added.

She nodded and typed a bit. "Well, you're a clean slate, then!"

I didn't like the perky tone of her voice. She made it sound like I was a mindless drone the United could program however they wanted.

Sadly, that was probably the case.

The principal submitted the application and spun her chair back around to face me. "You're all set! You're dismissed." She sounded so nonchalant about it, like a dental receptionist happily sending a patient off with clean teeth.

"Thank you, ma'am," I said as I rose. "And goodbye."

She didn't respond to that as I slipped out the door.

I slinked back to my classroom. I walked in to hear our teacher lecturing the few remaining unassimilated students about their duties as citizens, admonishing them not to be a deplorable failure like me. My friends Cami and Aid shared a gleeful glance and then winked in my direction.

As I sat down, the teacher wrinkled his nose at me like I was a species of pest that refused to be exterminated.

"Remember your former students, Mira and Stanyard. They accepted the wonderful opportunity the United offered them and went on to enjoy productive lives as free members of society," he said, staring at me as though he knew the comment would hurt me the most.

Cami and Aid stopped smirking. I hung my head and didn't look up again until the bell rang.

Lieutenant Clint picked us up from school in a United van. He was the new supervisor of our containment camp, having replaced Commander Ambrose who had been abruptly transferred a few months ago. One of the first things he had done upon taking control was to file a complaint that a full-size bus staffed with three armed guards was too much expense for the handful of elementary and high school students who still resided in our camp. Apparently his supervisors were more interested in saving money than they were in making a statement, because they had allowed him to start transporting us by himself in an unarmored van.

I liked the new arrangement. I had always enjoyed our brief sojourn across the Outside every day, but I enjoyed it even more now that our ride didn't turn heads, as the overgrown bus with the condemning words ASSIMILATION SERVICES splayed on the side had.

Being the oldest and therefore presumably bravest, I volunteered to sit shotgun next to the lieutenant. Normally he did not talk to us except to take a headcount or impart United announcements, but today he glanced at me as he navigated the harried late-afternoon traffic.

"Are you officially graduated now?"

"Yes," I replied, tensing and waiting to see if he would be scornful.

"Did you apply to the employment program?"

"Yes."

He nodded and turned back to face the road. "Good. I'll see what I can do to arrange for a job for you."

"Thank you," I said, mostly as a way to close the conversation. I wasn't sure how I felt about the lieutenant taking a personal interest in me. If Commander Ambrose had arranged a job for me, I would have been very wary that it was part of some scheme to get me—or my father—to sign. But Lieutenant Clint had so far shown himself to be more realistic, if not disinterested.

But why was he offering to arrange a job for me when he had not yet secured one for my father?

Maybe today was the day. Maybe today he had found something, and my father and brother would meet me at the door with excited smiles. Or better yet, maybe today they wouldn't be home to meet me at all, having gone for orientation at their new job.

That line of thought was the only way I could justify feeling disappointed when Daddy opened the door to meet me as I approached the step of our concrete home.

"Congratulations on your graduation," he said with a smile—the first proud smile I had received all day, and the only one I needed.

I beamed and hugged him. He returned the affection with a kiss on the top of my head.

"No news?" I prodded as we went inside.

He shook his head but retained a chipper tone. "Nothing today, but we have some new leads."

"What he means is none of the labs in this region want us, so Clint is going to ask all the labs in the neighboring districts," my brother Ephesus quipped from the kitchen. We came around the corner to find him sitting at the table, scowling at his laptop.

"Let's not talk about that tonight," Daddy said firmly. "We have a graduation to celebrate." He squeezed my shoulders, and I grinned.

Ephesus flashed a quick smile at me but kept talking. "I can't imagine the United will approve our transfer to another camp, though, and I desperately hope they'd consider commuting too much of an expense. We'd never be home if we had to commute that far."

I didn't like the idea of transferring, or of my only family being gone any more than they had to, but where else could they go for work? "Have you reapplied to the chemical research lab?" I said with weak hope. "Maybe now that the investigation with Dr. Nic has been completed, they'll let you back in…"

Ephesus was shaking his head despondently before I even finished.

"But the lab always wanted you before," I pouted, flopping down next to him. I thought of the long hours and special assignments that had kept them away so often in the past. What had changed?

"That was before we worked on Red Rain," Ephesus snapped.

"But it wasn't your project! You were… working against your will," I fumbled, not sure how to say it without offending him—or bringing back painful memories.

"Yeah, and I think that's the only reason they're not prosecuting me as an insurrectionist like they did with Nic." Ephesus crossed his arms and glanced away, but not before I saw the flicker of guilt in his eyes.

Daddy sat down with us at the table and touched Ephesus's shoulder. "We should just be grateful that no further trouble came from it."

Ephesus relaxed and unfolded his arms, but he didn't turn to look at us.

"But what about you?" I asked, looking imploringly at Daddy. "You didn't work on the project."

Daddy's expression was calm. "I was still involved."

Even though I knew he was being sensible, I couldn't copy his complacency. "But you were on the United's side! You turned Dr. Nic in."

"No, I didn't. You did."

I stared at him.

A proud smile lifted his lips as he said, "You're the one that stalled Dr. Nic and called the authorities."

"Yeah," Ephesus piped up, "you're the good little Unionist. If there's anyone they'll be fond of, it's you."

I glanced at him, and he winked. I couldn't bring myself to smile back, even though I knew he was teasing. I didn't like comparing myself to a compliant Unionist.

"Does that mean they'll probably give me a job?" I asked, turning back to Daddy. The United had never given me any recognition for turning in Dr. Nic except to question me briefly about the events. Was it possible my involvement had made a favorable mark on my file?

Daddy reached across the table and found my hand. "I don't know. But I do know that you'll be rewarded for your work one day, even if it isn't by the United." He squeezed my hand and smiled.

I smiled back.

2

We celebrated my graduation with the only thing we had available to us—food. Ephesus, unable to work with his beloved chemicals in the lab, had turned to mixing spices as a way to keep his hands busy. While I was gone at school, he had turned out a rather impressive dinner and a darling little frosted cake, which we enjoyed with much laughter around the table.

After dinner, Ephesus excused himself to his bedroom, gleefully saying he had to "wrap gifts." He returned with a cloth draped over his hand just as Daddy and I were finishing up the dishes. "Your graduation present, dear sister," he declared, yanking the cloth off with more flourish than was necessary. My beloved old reader lay on his palm.

Apprehension damped my excitement. "What did you do to it?"

"Look at your Bible study notes and see," he said with a grin.

Taking the warm device in my hands, I quickly navigated the menus to my study folder. My jumbled note documents had been replaced by an application titled "Study Reflections." With a sideways glance at my brother, I opened it and discovered all my notes had been filed and organized into one program.

"Now your study notes are all in one place, and you can search through them. And look, you can sort them by passage, or date, or keyword…" Unable to contain his excitement any longer, Ephesus leaned over my shoulder and pawed through options so rapidly I couldn't keep up with him.

"Wow," I managed, which was usually the only thing I could find to say in response to my brother's expert programming.

Knowing that was a genuine compliment coming from me, Ephesus stood back with a grin. "It's a gift from Cea and me."

"'Cea *and* me'?" I repeated, looking up at him.

He nodded eagerly. "We made it together," he said with a strange smile I didn't know how to interpret.

I glanced sideways at Daddy, but his face held no particular expression. "So *that's* what you two have been working on for the past few weeks," I edged casually, thinking of all the times I had come home to find Ephesus and Cea bent over the computer with their heads together. Sometimes she came in the evening and stayed unduly late into the night.

Ephesus shrugged. "Some of it," he said, and offered no further explanation.

"What else do you suppose they've been working on?" I asked Daddy after Ephesus had wandered off a little while later.

"I don't know," Daddy said with just the slightest hint of concern.

Glancing around to make sure Ephesus wasn't within earshot, I voiced the thought I had been harboring for several weeks. "Do you think there's… something going on between them?"

"I don't *think* so…" Daddy's eyebrows knotted together in a disgruntled expression I found more amusing than worrisome. I couldn't help but smile.

He shook his head and rose from the table. "Come on. I have something for you, too."

I followed him up to his bedroom. I stood back and watched while he got down on the floor—an action which looked surprisingly painful—and dragged something out from the farthest corner under the bed.

I involuntarily gasped when I recognized the small purple carry-on. *Mama's suitcase.*

Daddy hoisted it onto the bed with a sigh. "This was hers," he said, even though I didn't need to be told. "It was the suitcase she brought when we were first taken to the camp."

I remembered that day. It was almost six years ago now, when the soldiers forced us to pack and move into the concentration camps. One suitcase per person had been the rule. My mother had been the wisest packer; there were still things I regretted not bringing with me, and others I wish I had left behind.

Daddy unzipped the suitcase. "Everything that's left of hers I saved in here." I dared to step closer and look over his shoulder.

He opened the flap to reveal a meticulously-packed stack of clothes interspersed with other personal items. He took the objects out one by one, arranging them on the bed. I reached out to gingerly finger a floral skirt, remembering how it had looked fluttering around Mama's ankles as she danced about the kitchen.

"I want you to have everything." Daddy's voice was hushed, but his sudden declaration still startled me.

I turned to face him. "Me?"

His eyes were on the suitcase as he nodded. "Some of it might fit you now. Here, try these on." He pulled a pair of shoes from the bottom of the suitcase and set them on the floor.

It was a pair of black suede flats, simple yet pretty. I stared at them for a moment before I pulled my socks off and gingerly slipped my pale feet into them. They fit like Cinderella's glass slippers.

I looked up into my father's face. He was staring at me, but with an expression that made me wonder if he wasn't really seeing *me* anymore.

"You really do look just like her," he commented, more to himself than to me.

I waited. Surely he hadn't given me all this just because I could wear some of it.

He sighed, voice returning to normal. "I was going to save this for your eighteenth birthday, but I think today is a more appropriate occasion."

He looked into my face, eyes clearly focused on me now. "Today, in the eyes of the United, you became an adult. Up until now you have been under the authority of your parents and your teachers. We have raised you, and the United has attempted to train you. You have been given a foundation, tools, and beliefs with which to design your future."

He paused and laid his hands on my shoulders. "Now it is up to you to decide what to build."

I studied his expression, waiting.

"From today on, your identity is your own. Your circumstances do not dictate what path you choose for yourself. The United respects that and hopes you will use that opportunity to join their ranks."

I snorted. Daddy smiled, but he nudged my chin and forced me to look back up at him. "I, too, respect your freedom."

I frowned. Daddy's eyes were full of loving severity as he continued. "I have given you a choice just like the United has. I cannot make that choice for you. Even while you are living with me under my roof, I cannot force you to accept my beliefs as your own."

A pressure, a feeling close to grief, filled my heart, even though I couldn't explain why. The warmth in Daddy's voice only made it heavier. "It has given me great joy to see you follow God's path this far, to make the right choices even without my encouragement. But from here on out your choices will become even more important. Your life will no longer be regulated by school and the constant oversight of your teachers. You will have freedom and opportunities, and you will have to decide what to do with those opportunities. And one day…"

He hesitated, and pain clogged his voice and clouded his eyes. "And... there may be times when I am not with you. The decision is always yours, but the time may come when I am not even able to give you counsel. If you get a job, you will be out in the world, faced with temptation, and I won't be within arm's reach. There might not be anyone you can turn to."

The pressure in my heart started to make my eyes burn. Daddy's eyes were openly watering as he pulled me into a tight hug. "I love you, Philadelphia," he whispered in my ear. "I love the beautiful young lady you have become. But only you can decide to continue to grow up and become a strong woman like your mother."

Like my mother. How I wanted that! How I wanted to be brave like her, so brave that I would die for my beliefs—and so godly that everyone would remember me as a beacon of hope, a reminder of why we kept fighting.

I took a deep breath, suddenly finding the courage to voice a proposition I had been praying over for weeks. Standing back from my father, I declared in the most mature voice I could muster, "Daddy, I want to transmit."

His first reaction was a confused frown. "You already give copies to your friends. There isn't much else you can do from camp."

"I know, but if I get a job in the Outside, there could be an opportunity for me to transmit from work. Just like you used to. Just like... Mama." I looked up into his face.

He regarded me with a sad but dry expression, the expression of hardened grief. "You know your mother died for that," he said, which was what I had expected him to say.

"I know." I could still remember the exact words he'd said to me when I came home from school that day. His voice had been calculated, as if he had spent all day preparing what to say.

"They came to investigate charges of transmitting Bibles through the internet. She was brave and honest and wouldn't deny it." I'd interrupted his prepared speech and demanded to

know what they'd done with her. He'd been forced to admit very plainly: *"They took her away. They said she'll be executed."*

I denied it. For three weeks I hotly insisted that she couldn't be dead. Daddy quietly insisted that she was. My young, grieved mind found a million ways to refute his statement. How would he know? They *said* they were going to execute her, but what if they didn't? What if she was pardoned? What if she escaped?

I spent three weeks waiting for her to come home, and three weeks begging the guards, my teachers, and even Commander Ambrose for information. I even went behind Daddy's back to ask the neighbors what they saw, hoping they would contradict my father's claim.

Everyone told me she was gone. But it wasn't until I found traces of blood splatter on the wall in the entryway that I truly believed it. There were only a few drops, as though my father had tried to clean it up, but I knew what it was.

Then I understood how my father could be so resigned. He had seen her die. They hadn't taken her away to be executed; they had executed her right then and there, shot her for confessing to transmitting.

After that I stopped asking questions about Mama's death. But I didn't stop transmitting, copying Bibles to give to my fellow inmates when they needed them. Father hadn't stopped either; he had continued to transmit onto the internet from work until he lost his job.

And I wanted to continue the task for him.

He sighed again, an almost wistful sigh this time. He stroked a hand through my hair, his eyes glazing over again. "I'll think about it," he said finally.

Shaking his head to clear the fog from his expression, he straightened and forcibly brightened his voice. "Now, you run along downstairs and have fun. It's your day to celebrate."

I scrunched my nose. Exactly what did he expect me to have fun doing?

A knowing smile tugged at his lips. "Go downstairs and you'll see."

I obeyed, giving him one last smile over my shoulder.

I skipped downstairs and nearly collided with my surprise—Cea, who was standing in the entryway talking to Ephesus.

"There's our special graduate!" she declared, turning around with a grin. "Congrats on surviving the system, girl."

I chuckled. "Thanks."

She brushed her cropped blond hair behind her ears. "How about a sleepover at my place?"

"A sleepover?" I repeated.

"Yeah! You know… Haven't you ever had a slumber party?"

I gave her a look that clearly said I hadn't.

She gaped at me. "You *are* sheltered."

Ephesus came to my defense. "It's not like there's anyone to party with around here. A sleepover isn't much of an event if it's just across the street."

"Oh, you're no fun." Cea flapped her hand at him. "Come on, grab your jammies and toothbrush. I've got Cami over too, and it will be just us girls all night."

I was still unsure about the whole concept. "Well, I have to ask my dad…" I turned around to find him standing at the bottom of the stairs, holding out my duffel.

"All packed," he said with an encouraging smile. "Have fun."

I couldn't help but laugh as I took the bag from him. "Guess I don't really have a choice, then."

"Nope!" Cea chirped, grabbing my arm. "Come on!" Then she dragged me out the door and across the street before I could even give my family a proper goodbye.

Cami was already there, in her pajamas and nearly buried in a pile of blankets and pillows in front of Cea's TV. "Philli!" she called in greeting, bouncing on a pillow. "Isn't it awesome? We're going to watch a movie! Cea even made popcorn!"

"A movie?" I said, trying to hide the skepticism in my voice. Ever since the United had started regulating media, most movies had ceased to be worth watching.

"Yup!" Cea said, clearly sharing Cami's excitement. "Ephesus finally figured out how to hack the DRM lock on the disc drive of my laptop so it can read old discs."

"Your laptop can play uncensored discs?" I cried with no small amount of alarm. "That's—"

"Yeah, and your reader has an illegal Bible on it," she returned.

I snapped my mouth shut.

She glanced back at me as she untangled some cords. "Your dad said it was okay."

At that, I relinquished and permitted myself to change into my pajamas and join Cami on the floor.

Cea hooked her laptop up to the TV and then showed us her secret collection. I didn't recognize any of the titles, so I let Cea pick which movie to watch. It ended up being a cute animated story about a clownfish who went on a great search to find his son after the little fish was caught by some divers. I liked it; the daddy fish reminded me of my father. He, too, would do anything to keep our little family together, now that Mama was gone.

Cami was practically out before the movie finished, but Cea and I were still wide awake. Cea let me look at the other discs before she put them away; I couldn't resist the urge to twirl one around my fingers and watch the dim light reflect off the shiny surface.

It had been a long time since I'd seen a disc. Grandpa used to have a whole collection of vintage movies on various disc formats, all in the original cases. I remembered sitting in front of the shelf, reading the titles and looking at the little pictures on the spines. I used to imagine what the story was about based on the picture. I hadn't seen any of Grandpa's movies; it was a collection and not for touching.

That just made it all the more tragic when the United had raided his house and seized his collection, snapping all the discs in half and tossing them in a dumpster.

"How did you smuggle these into camp?" I asked.

"Mostly in books," she replied, not looking up from her laptop screen. "I had more at the base. I brought them up before the United started collecting uncensored media, and they never bothered to come looking on Mars."

I nodded and tucked the disc carefully back in between the pages of an old dictionary. I fingered the spine for a moment before I dared to ask, "Have you heard anything about Nic yet?"

"No," was the sad reply. "Nothing."

"Have you asked the lieutenant if he can find out for you, since you're family?" I suggested hopefully.

Cea shook her head. "I did, and even he couldn't find any information. It's bizarre... It's not like it's confidential. It's like Nic never existed."

I frowned. Cea turned around to face me. "I can't find anything in the news, not even on the Martian sites, about his arrest. There's nothing linking him to the virus. His file hasn't had any new entries since he was granted governorship of the base. Even my file only says I was sentenced to containment because it was discovered I did not have the necessary paperwork and I refused to sign. That's a lie," she added rather indignantly. "I had signed the papers years ago. I chose to turn myself in."

My mind scrambled for the logic behind it all. "What about my file?"

She shook her head. "Nothing. Your file has remained unchanged since you were contained. The only thing that has been added is your school grades."

So they didn't make note of the fact that I turned Dr. Nic in. This upset me, but not because I wasn't getting credit for my good deed. There was something more, but I couldn't put my finger on it.

"Ephesus has hacked the camp's internet restrictions and managed to access some of the government criminal databases, but even he can't find any mentions of Nic or Red Rain or anything. It's like... it's like they don't want anyone to know what he did."

"Why?" I asked what we both were thinking. "Why wouldn't they make a big deal out of having arrested him? That's what they usually do with rebels. Make a spectacle out of their punishment to scare everyone else away from trying."

Cea shrugged. "The only thing I can think of is maybe they didn't want people to know how close he came to succeeding."

I nodded, shivering a little at the thought. Dr. Nic was good. He'd convinced the United—and my family—that my brother was dead, maintained a secret server of dangerous research, and released a virus that had wiped a significant chunk of Earth's data. And even if Red Rain remained unfinished, he had built a startling array of other weapons without ever arousing the United's suspicion.

Cea turned back to her computer. "Ephesus will keep digging. But we're beginning to wonder if they've given Nic a code name to conceal the records."

She resumed typing. I took my hair out of its ponytail and twisted it around my fingers, debating how hard I wanted to push the subject. "Is that what you two have been working on? Hacking around the internet controls?"

"Some of it," she replied without looking up. "We're working on a few other projects too."

"Like what?" I asked, hoping I sounded curious and not accusatory.

"Stuff for the future." She kept typing.

I wrinkled my nose in confusion. "The future?"

She finally looked at me. "You don't expect us to stay in this camp forever, do you?"

I stared at her. No one had ever asked me that, except the United, who excepted me to deny my religion and join their order.

And Stanyard and Mira. They had said something like that to me before they left. I remembered Mira's painful voice shrieking angrily at me. *We're not going to do it anymore! We're leaving! We're not going to keep living stuffed away in a little hole until they decide to kill us.*

I swallowed. What choice did we have but to stay here? The only other option was to join them.

Cea frowned. "There are other options, Phil." Her voice was condescending. "We don't have to sit quietly here and play their game. Ephesus and I won't."

I wasn't sure how to respond to that. Thankfully she didn't expect an answer and returned to her typing.

I buried my chin in my pillow, trying to fight the dread that filled my stomach. I wasn't even sure what was upsetting me. Maybe it was the accusation in Cea's voice. Maybe it was my worry over what other "options" she and Ephesus might be working on.

What did she expect us to do? Staying in the camp meant we got to keep practicing our religion without interference. Maybe it wouldn't last, but in the meantime, where else could we go? Breaking out of the camp would put us on the run and in danger of our lives, unless we intended to fight back to maintain our independence—like Dr. Nic had.

And I didn't like that idea at all.

3

The knock came during dinner.

I think all three of us jumped. It was rare for us to get visitors, especially late at night. The fact that they were knocking—pounding, more like it—rather than using our obnoxious doorbell made it even stranger. We were so surprised that all three of us stood up and went to see who it was.

Ephesus answered the door. He had barely pulled it open before three armed guards shoved their way inside.

"May I help you?" Ephesus yelped indignantly, stumbling back.

The soldiers spread themselves in the entryway and halted. "We have orders to take two unassimilated citizens into special custody," the captain of the group declared.

I gasped, a sound which seemed gratingly loud in the sudden silence. For a moment it seemed the only thing moving in the entire room was my panicked heart.

Special custody... two unassimilated...

"What?" Ephesus yelled, more as an exclamation of shock than a question.

Dear God, no.

The captain ignored him. He scanned the room, his eyes coming to rest just above my head. I knew in my heart that he was looking at Daddy, who was standing behind me.

Please no...

I didn't have time to finish the prayer before the captain confirmed my fears. "You're under arrest."

God, no! Please don't take my father and brother away. Not again!

I whipped around to look at Daddy, silently begging him to tell me it wasn't true. Shock and fear briefly flashed across his eyes, but he let it out with a sigh. Straightening, he said with brave calmness, "Will you allow us to gather a few belongings first?"

The captain nodded. "Ten minutes."

Daddy turned towards the stairs. I yearned to cry out after him, but I couldn't find any words.

Ephesus stayed where he was and sputtered, "What is the meaning of this?"

The captain finally looked at him. "The reasons for her arrest are confidential."

Silence again iced over the room. This time my heart stopped altogether.

"Her?" Ephesus repeated.

Daddy stopped at the bottom of the stairs and glanced back.

"Yes," the captain said slowly, as if he didn't understand what the confusion was. "She's the one under arrest."

The statement was accompanied by a flick of his hand at me.

I gasped again, the sound catching in my throat like I was gagging. I slapped my hand over my mouth, afraid a worse sound would escape.

The captain glared at me. "Ten minutes. Hurry up."

Ephesus shook himself and resumed sputtering. "But what did she do?"

"That's confidential," the captain repeated with condescending patience.

Ephesus continued to argue, but I couldn't understand what he was saying. My head spun. *What... why... where...* I couldn't even formulate a complete question.

"Daddy," I managed. I turned towards him, groping for an explanation.

Wordlessly he grabbed my hand and hauled me up the stairs. He pulled me into my room and shut the door behind us.

Turning to me, he started talking swiftly but clearly. "I don't know what they want you for, but we'll find out. Don't worry—special custody doesn't mean anything."

My head and heart were throbbing too much for me to obey the admonition not to worry, but I did my best to focus on his instructions around the whirlwind.

He strode to the closet and fetched Mama's purple suitcase. I wished he had grabbed my old duffel instead—something about using Mama's suitcase made it seem more serious, more final—as if we were both silently agreeing that this was something I wouldn't come back from. But I couldn't find the words to voice my pathetic fears.

He started moving methodically around the room, scooping items into the case with purpose. "It just means something's come up that the United wants to look into. That's how they are—if there's any suspicion, they take people into special custody until they can investigate. They probably just want to talk to you. Just answer their questions honestly and it will be okay. You've already been contained for being unassimilated; you can't have done anything that will warrant a punishment worse than a warning and getting sent back here."

"But I haven't done anything at all!" I cried, some of my panicked thoughts escaping. "They haven't even given me a job yet!"

He glanced back at me as he moved into the Jack-and-Jill bathroom. "I know. But that probably means there's nothing wrong and they'll send you back here."

As much as I tried to absorb his calm demeanor, I did not find words such as "probably" to be comforting. What if there was something wrong? Something I couldn't deny?

"Hopefully it won't take long." At this, even Daddy's confidence wavered; I could hear it in his voice. He looked down and shoveled the contents of my bathroom drawer into the bag. "But if there's a wait, you'll have your belongings. Your belongings will have to be inspected by security, though. You'll speed up the process if you don't take any suspicious items—no electronics."

I involuntarily glanced towards my reader, which lay on the nightstand. *But my Bible...*

"Don't worry," he said again, and I still couldn't take it to heart. "It's not like being put in prison. You'll probably be taken to something like an apartment building where you'll wait until the local officials can see you."

Being confined in solitude, ripped from my family without any explanation, sounded a lot like prison to me.

"This should tide you over." He zipped the suitcase shut and dropped it on the bed, then walked over to me.

I looked up at him, searching for something more. Some reassurance, some admonition, some token of wisdom. Something that would give me his confidence, his peace. He had been in this kind of situation before; he knew exactly what to say, what to do, when to bend, and when to stand firm. I wanted to be like him. I wanted to do the right thing—so that no one would get hurt.

Daddy suddenly seemed at a loss for words too. He gazed at me for a moment, the kind of loving stare that indicated he was studying me, pondering thoughts that only fathers know.

I wanted to say goodbye—I wanted him to say goodbye—but I knew that neither of us could come up with the words.

Finally, Daddy scooped my jacket off my desk chair and held it up. I numbly slid into it. It did nothing to warm the chill tingling down my arms.

"Behave. Be polite." Daddy absentmindedly zipped my coat as he talked. "Obey the rules. Don't cause trouble."

I swallowed. I remembered the last time he had recited that exact same list—when we were standing on the porch waiting for Commander Ambrose to take Daddy to the airport. The day Daddy was supposed to be flying to Mars on business, forced to leave me behind. The day I was supposed to go live with the Nolans, not knowing if I would ever see my father again.

Tears suddenly shot to my eyes.

"Oh, Philli." Daddy reached out and pulled me into a hug. I tried to dam the tears, to trust, to pray, but the brokenhearted tone of his voice only made me panic more. I sobbed and grabbed him around the neck.

"Oh, Philadelphia," he said again. "I'm sorry." He kissed my cheek and stroked my hair, pressing my face against his chest. I let myself sob, tears and prayers spilling freely.

Suddenly I felt him stiffen, and he jerked away. "Come on."

His tone had changed to one of hard determination. I stared in confusion as he grabbed my arm with one hand and my bag with the other. He dragged me out of the room and down the stairs. I stumbled along behind, sniffing to swallow the tears.

Ephesus's urgent voice reached us from the front room. "Can't you tell us anything, off the record?"

"Nothing happens off the record," was the blunt reply.

"But she hasn't done anything wrong! She's always been compliant."

With a wince, I realized that he wasn't being completely truthful. I wasn't violent, but I wasn't always compliant. I was a transmitter. I copied illegal Bibles. Was that what they wanted me for? Had Commander Clint decided to crack down on my distribution and charge me with transmitting?

Were they going to execute me just like they'd done with Mama?

Ephesus's voice was getting dangerously heated, like a chemical reaction about to explode. "She's the one that told you about Red Rain! She could have let Nic scald you to death, but she decided to turn him in even though she knew you'd send her back to a concentration camp! How can you say—"

"Sirs," my father interrupted, stepping into the room.

The group of soldiers turned their faces and guns towards us. The captain nodded and beckoned at me, but Daddy stepped between us.

"Please," he said, "allow me to accompany her."

I stiffened, hope sending a jolt up my spine. I squeezed Daddy's hand, praying desperately.

The captain drew his eyebrows together, as if unsure what to make of that request. Daddy continued, "I will gladly join her wherever she is being sent."

Ephesus glanced between us, then raised his hand. "I could go also."

I shook my head at him. As much as I didn't want to choose between them, this was a time I needed Daddy.

The captain shook his head. "That's against regulations. Come on." He reached towards me.

Daddy shoved me further behind him. "Please, she's a minor." Daddy's voice was rising in panic, and his words became less formal. "Whatever you want her for, I'll come with her. I will take whatever punishment—"

"No." The captain's voice took on a commanding edge I knew all too well. "She's the one under arrest, not you."

It's his assignment, not yours. Regulations. Another sob escaped my throat unbidden.

Suddenly I was in Daddy's arms again. He kissed me and muttered quickly in my ear, "I love you. Remember me. Remember your mother. Remember God."

The blood was pounding in my ears so hard I could barely hear him. I opened my arms to hug him, but someone else grabbed my hand. A soldier yanked me so fast I stumbled backwards. Another gripped my other arm, hauled me up, and shoved me towards the door.

"Philli!" Ephesus cried.

I turned towards him, but there were soldiers on all sides of me. I opened my mouth to call out to him, but the soldiers pushed me forward again. I tripped on the threshold and crashed down the front steps. I yelled as my leg scraped on the concrete. I landed on my knees on the sidewalk.

"Careful!" someone barked.

Soldiers tromped down the steps. I sensed them around me, but I couldn't move. I just knelt there, pain and blood coursing from my torn shin.

An arm appeared in my peripheral vision. I looked up to see a guard bending over me with his hand outstretched. As much as I didn't want to go with him, instinct made me reach out and accept his offer of help.

He pulled me to my feet and straightened into the light of the streetlamp, allowing me to make out his face. He was young, not that much older or taller than myself, with a tidy red-orange goatee. "Are you all right?" he said in a bright voice, not seeming at all impatient.

"Yeah," I said. It was a lie, I realized as I put pressure on my scraped leg, but I appreciated the kind question. "Thank you."

He nodded and, still holding onto my arm, guided me towards the windowless van idling on the street. I was glad to be walking rather than dragged, so I went willingly.

He was just about to help me step up into the back of the van when the captain approached. "Blindfold her," he ordered without ceremony.

"But why?" I cried, all the terror resurging in my mind.

"The general doesn't want her and the other prisoner to meet," the captain said, more to the guard holding my arm than to me. He held up a strip of black cloth.

I shied. The young guard holding my arm didn't move, but he didn't reach out to take the cloth, either. "In that case, sir, perhaps she should sit up with us in the cab, and the other can ride in the back. Then they won't hear each other's voices."

I turned and looked back at him in surprise. Was he showing me mercy?

The captain considered that for a moment, then retracted his hand and put the cloth in his pocket. "Fine. But keep a gun trained on her."

He turned and walked across the street. I tried to see which house he was going to, but my escort tugged on my arm and pulled me around to the front of the van. "This way."

He opened the door and spotted me while I climbed into the back seat of the cab. There was no one else in the cab except for a surly driver who spared only two seconds to glance over his shoulder at me before returning his attention to his phone.

The young guard hopped into the front seat beside him with the careless agility of a teenager climbing into his friend's pickup for a joyride. Shutting the door, he tossed his gun, which he evidently had no intention of pointing at me, on the dashboard and propped his boots up beside it.

Leaning back against the seat, he turned his head to face me. "Jayde," he offered. "Is Philli short for something?"

"Philadelphia," I replied.

"That's a long one," he said with an amused puff of breath. I just waited, wondering how far his friendliness would go.

He propped his arm on the back of the seat. "So what are you in for?"

I swallowed. "I don't know…"

"I mean, here in a camp," he quickly clarified. "Are you in for religious reasons?"

"Oh, yes," I said, relieved at the change of conversation.

He nodded. "Thought so. This place is too low security for anything else. But don't tell anyone I told you that; they'll accuse me of helping you escape." He guffawed and jabbed the driver in the shoulder. The driver only responded with an eye roll.

I stared at him, not at all sure what to make of the conversation. If our camp was low security, what did high security look like? Were they taking me somewhere with higher security? Why? I had never tried to escape.

"So what religion are you?" he continued his casual query.

"Christian," I said, wondering what that term would mean to him.

"Figures," he responded shortly. I couldn't tell if he sounded annoyed, bored, or completely disinterested.

Before I could ask what he meant by that, shouting outside interrupted us. The van rocked roughly.

Jayde turned around in his seat and picked up his gun. "Guess they got the other one."

I winced, hoping the other prisoner wasn't being treated roughly. Who were they? There weren't that many people left in camp. Who could it be? What had they done? Why didn't the officials want us to meet each other? Did they suspect us of being in crime together?

An order was shouted outside, and Jayde buckled his seatbelt. "Let's go," he said.

The driver reluctantly pocketed his device and started the engine. I hastily found my seatbelt and buckled it.

The van lurched to an ungraceful start and lumbered out of the camp. I scooted up to the window and watched, taking in the scenery like I had done while riding to and from school. It had been a long time since I had seen the city at night, and gazing in childlike wonder at the passing lights distracted me from the fact that we were driving *away* from camp and not towards it.

It did not take long for us to reach our destination. Daddy was right—the place did look like an apartment building. It was an altogether boring structure that blended in perfectly with the other shapeless high rises on the street. The only visible sign was the generic United seal with the words "Office No. 32.8" emblazoned in metal above the door.

Despite the unassuming appearance of the building, I still caught myself swallowing repeatedly in fear as we drove down the ramp into the parking garage below.

As soon as we stopped, Jayde jumped out and opened the door for me. I stepped down and looked towards the back of the van, hoping to catch a glance of the other prisoner.

Jayde seemed to have been ordered to prevent exactly that, however, and pulled me away at such an angle to keep me from being able to see in the back of the van.

He led me to an elevator which took us up an alarming number of floors. I began to feel dizzy, though whether from the height or the dread accumulating in my mind, I couldn't tell.

Finally the elevator stopped. The doors opened to reveal a long, sterile, gray-painted hall, lined further than I could see with numbered doors.

Hefty body scanners stood guard on either side of the elevator doors. Jayde instructed me to walk through them slowly. After a second of irate buzzing, the scanners flashed a bright, welcoming green.

I found the irony of that absolutely sickening.

Jayde led me to the third door on the right. He opened it with a flick of his fingers across the security panel.

The room beyond was dark, but thankfully Jayde stepped in ahead of me and turned the lights on. *It's just like an apartment. Nothing scary about a dorm room,* I reminded myself. Taking a deep breath, I willingly stepped into the room.

My heart sank at the sight of it. The room was small, and worse, it was bare. It had a low cot, a rickety card table with two chairs, a narrow bathroom, and an even narrower locker. There were no windows, and everything was made out of cold, hard metal.

Metal. So much metal.

"I can't bring your baggage up tonight. It has to be approved by security," Jayde said from behind me, sounding apologetic.

My heart sank even further.

"If you need anything, press the star button and it will alert a guard."

I didn't answer. Jayde didn't seem to expect a response and stepped back, closing the door.

The familiar beep and *woosh* of air struck my nerves. I spun around and stared at the panel by the door. It looked exactly like the technology they'd had in the base on Mars—technology I had been able to circumvent.

I ran to the door and pressed my hand over the sensor.

The hideous beep pierced my ears, making them ring.

Access denied.

I stumbled backwards and tripped over the cot. Sitting down hard, I stared at the red *X* until it faded away.

The ringing in my ears subsided, leaving me completely alone in the silence. I dropped back on the cot and pulled my knees up. And then I allowed myself to cry.

4

A buzzing stirred me from my sleep. I laid still for a moment, blinking the haze out of my eyes. The lights were on full blast. Why was I sleeping with the lights on?

The buzzing continued erratically, like someone was ringing a doorbell repeatedly. I lifted my head and looked around, then remembered. It *was* a doorbell—the doorbell to my tiny cell.

I groaned and wondered if prisoners were allowed to ignore their doorbells. Figuring I'd better not push boundaries on the first day, I dragged myself out of bed.

I yelped as soon as I stood up. My right leg burned. I lifted my skirt and realized my shin was clotted with a delightfully large scab. I'd forgotten about scraping my leg on the concrete last night.

Sighing, I stepped forward—and tripped over the chair. I crashed into the door, narrowly managing to miss hitting buttons on the control panel. I growled, feeling more annoyed at my own clumsiness than anything else.

Shaking my head to clear it, I reached up and pushed the call button. "Who is it?"

"Jayde," was the answer from a male voice. Then, as if realizing that name meant nothing to me, he added, "The guard from last night."

After a moment's thought, I was able to recall his face, and while I was glad it was him and not some surly guard who didn't even know my name, I still wasn't sure I was up for another friendly chat with him. I leaned my head against the door, trying to think of a way to ask what he wanted without being rude. Daddy said be polite, and I didn't want to get in trouble for being snappy.

Thankfully, Jayde volunteered the information. "I came to see if you needed anything."

I straightened. "What time is it?"

"Umm…" There was a pause. "8:30," he answered finally. "Can I get you anything?"

"Umm…" It was my turn to stall. I glanced around the room, trying to decide what I even wanted. "Some breakfast would be nice," I decided.

"It's already on its way. Anything else?"

"Not really…" I shifted my weight and winced as the tender skin on my leg stretched. "Actually, I think I'm going to need a bandage for my leg."

"Oh, they forgot to look at that last night?" He let out a low whistle. I wondered if someone was going to get in trouble for the oversight. "I'll get the nurse. Be right back."

I would have thanked him, but his footsteps were already pounding down the hall. I shut off the call and turned back to the room. I took a minute to straighten the blanket on the cot and tidy my appearance as best I could without my toiletries. I didn't want to look like a prisoner that had been sleeping in the king's dungeon for a week. Hopefully the officers would approve my baggage soon.

My doorbell buzzed ten minutes later. I went to open it, then remembered I couldn't. Cringing, I pressed the call button and said, "Come in."

I backed out of the way as the door opened. Jayde appeared with a breakfast tray in one hand and my suitcase in the other. "Here's your breakfast." He set the tray down on the table. "And your baggage has been cleared. Everything was fine." He tossed my bag on the chair.

"Thank you," I said, mentally directing the same at God.

A second set of footsteps approached the open door. "Here's the nurse," Jayde said.

Before I could turn, a voice I remembered all too clearly rang out.

"Oh, Philadelphia, sweetheart!"

I wasn't sure whether to cringe or gasp in shock. I managed to turn my head and look at her.

Mrs. Nolan looked exactly like she had on the day she'd come to visit me at school, wanting me to come live with her. Her hair was cropped and perfectly styled, and her cheeks were painted a doll-like shade of pink. The only difference was that she was wearing a prim white uniform with a shiny name badge instead of casual jeans and a t-shirt.

She looked almost as shocked as I felt. She stared at me for several minutes like I was a ghost from her past. Then all at once she started gushing, voice as buttery as ever.

"Oh, you poor thing! Whatever are you doing here? Did they hurt you? Oh, sweetheart." She dropped her supply bag and bustled towards me. I involuntarily stepped back.

Jayde glanced between us. "Do you need any assistance?" he asked Mrs. Nolan.

"Oh no, she won't be any trouble at all. She's such a sweet and polite dear, aren't you?" Mrs. Nolan crooned.

Jayde arched his eyebrows and looked at me. I almost begged him to stay behind for *my* sake.

Smirking with obvious amusement, Jayde turned to go. "Call if you need anything," he said as he shut the door behind him.

I turned around just in time to see Mrs. Nolan come at me with a hug. "Oh darling, it's so good to see you again."

I couldn't return the sentiment, but I didn't refuse her hug. She squeezed me and then held me at arm's length. "Are you all right? What did they do to you?"

"I'm fine, ma'am, really," I said, hoping my sincerity would deter any further mothering. "I just tripped and scraped my leg on the way in." I lifted my skirt to show her.

She gasped. "Oh, look at that... Sit down." Her voice suddenly changed to one of authority, which I found much more comforting than her squeal. I obeyed, and she fetched her medical bag from the floor.

"We'll get that cleaned up." She pulled a sterile wipe out of her bag and started cleaning the wound. I was surprised at how swiftly and gently her hands worked.

She continued to interrogate me as she treated my injury, but her voice was less urgent than before. "How did you get here, sweetheart?"

"They took me last night," I answered. How else did one get into prison?

"What did you do?" She glanced up at me sideways as she fished some antibiotic cream out of her bag.

I blinked a few times. "I... don't know," I managed finally. "They wouldn't tell me. They just said I was under arrest and had to be taken into special custody."

Mrs. Nolan pouted. "That's just like them, the beasts. Terrifying innocent little girls for no reason."

I watched her rub the cream onto my leg. I wasn't going to tell her that one of the most terrifying things the United had ever done was try to send me to live with her.

She started wrapping my leg with a white bandage. "You don't deserve this. You'd never hurt anybody. I bet this is all a big mistake and it will be cleared up soon."

I had to admit that I found her words somewhat comforting. The United had a "shoot first, ask questions later" policy when it came to arresting people. There was a chance they were acting on suspicions and would soon figure out I wasn't a threat. But I was already in a concentration camp—what would drive them to put me under special custody?

As soon as Mrs. Nolan finished securing the bandage, her motherly fussing returned, and she took it upon herself to get me cleaned up. She made me wash my face, brush my teeth, style my hair, and change into an outfit she selected from my baggage. All the while she took the liberty of putting my belongings away in the little locker of my cell. I didn't like her interference at all, but I wasn't sure I was in a position to refuse her. I knew Daddy would want me to be lenient, at any rate.

She had just finished tidying the room to her satisfaction when the doorbell rang again. She opened it to reveal Jayde and two other guards, all armed.

"The captain has summoned you," he said, leaning over to look at me around Mrs. Nolan's plump frame.

Mixed fear and hope fluttered through my stomach. Maybe they would finally tell me what I had done wrong.

I stepped forward, but Mrs. Nolan blocked the doorway. "Oh heavens!" she blustered. I noted that was a rather odd expression for an Outsider, who was supposed to have no religion, to use. "You didn't even let the poor girl finish her breakfast."

I glanced back at the untouched meal and sighed.

Jayde scrunched his brow in a look that said, *"What have you been doing all this time?"* I shrugged helplessly.

Jayde shook his head. "He will see her now," he said firmly.

I nodded in consent, but Mrs. Nolan wagged her head, making her cropped hair flop about. "Don't give me that. You already terrorized the poor girl by dragging her here in the middle of the night—let her have something to eat! She's not going anywhere."

"He will see her—" Jayde started to repeat.

"No, she needs to eat. Doctor's orders." Mrs. Nolan flapped her hands at him. "You tell him I said that."

I gazed at her in wonder. I'd never seen an Outsider stand up to a soldier like that—and I'd never had anyone defend me in front of the United.

For the first time in my life, I thanked God for letting Mrs. Nolan take an interest in me.

To my surprise, Jayde backed away. "I'll tell him," he said, almost condescendingly. I assumed that meant he was going to blame Mrs. Nolan and let her face off with the captain. I swallowed and hoped neither of us was going to get in trouble for it.

As soon as the guards walked away, Mrs. Nolan turned back to me. "Never mind them. Now you eat up, every last bite. You need your strength."

"Yes, ma'am," I said with grateful obedience.

She beamed at me with her porcelain smile. "I wish I could stay, dear, but I need to go check on someone else. I think they came in with you last night—poor thing."

I stiffened. "Do you know who it is?"

"You haven't met them?" she said with an innocent frown, but thankfully she didn't wait for an answer. "I don't know, but I'm going to go find out!" She grinned and scooped up her medical bag.

A thought raced through my mind. I swallowed and ventured, "Will you… come back and visit me later?"

Her expression melted into one of deplorable pity. "Of course, darling."

She wrapped me in another hug. I forced myself to return it, feeling wickedly manipulative.

After Mrs. Nolan left, I sat down and ate hastily. I didn't want to bank on the captain listening to Mrs. Nolan and waiting for me to finish.

Surprisingly, Mrs. Nolan's orders were heeded, and the guards didn't come back for fifteen minutes. By that time, though, I had begun to regret eating before going to see the captain—the butterflies in my stomach made it difficult to even swallow.

Jayde led the way, with the other two guards following behind me. I tried to pretend that they weren't there and instead focused on Jayde, who walked with a lax confidence that I found somewhat comforting.

Jayde took us back to the elevator and up several more flights to a floor that looked vastly different than the one my cell was on. Instead of bland halls that looked horribly institutional, this floor was classy. It had wood-paneled walls, plush carpet, and potted plants interspersed between the gold-numbered doors. The wall on the right was entirely glass, allowing a brilliant view of the city. I squinted in the sudden onslaught of unfiltered daylight.

Jayde walked up to a door halfway down the hall and paged the occupants. Without waiting for a response, he said, "I've brought her, sir."

For an answer, the door beeped and opened. I found that welcome somewhat unsettling.

I took a gulp of air, trying one last time to swallow my queasiness, and bravely strode into the room without being bidden. Jayde followed me inside.

It was an unbelievably posh office. It was dominated by an intimidatingly large desk, behind which sat an equally intimidating, although not particularly large, man.

"You two are dismissed," he called out into the hall. The other two guards left with an obedient nod. Jayde closed and locked the door behind them. He took up station to the side of the door. Three military officers stood guard in the shadowy corners of the room.

The man behind the desk didn't move, probably because he was already sitting with precise posture. He wore a tailored and evidently expensive suit. He didn't look like a military officer, but he was clearly rich, which meant he almost assuredly had to be a United official of some kind. The decor of the room certainly reminded me of a politician's office.

"Sit, Philadelphia," he commanded in an unerringly calm voice.

I obeyed hastily, taking the closest chair. I suddenly felt clumsy compared to the man's perfect movements. I folded my hands in my lap in a vain attempt to maintain some delicacy.

"Thank you for your cooperation thus far," the politician said. He sounded genuine in his praise, but I wasn't sure how to respond to that.

He shifted ever so slightly to reach forward and stroke his fingers across the tablet lying on the desk in front of him. I heard a quiet tinkle and knew I was being recorded. I tried not to let that fact disturb me; the United was always recording everything no matter where you went.

"I need you to answer some questions for me," he said.

A breath of relief rushed into me as I recalled Daddy's words. *They probably just want to talk to you. Just answer their questions honestly and it will be okay.* I nodded and sat up a little straighter.

I could have imagined it, but I thought the man smiled at this. Folding his hands on the desk, he began, "I need you to tell us everything you know about the project called 'Red Rain.'"

My heart skipped at the familiar but near-forgotten name. Red Rain? Dr. Nic's pet project? Was that what this was all about?

Of course. It all made sense now. That's why Dr. Nic's arrest still hadn't been published in the news. They were investigating his operations and wanted to know more about my involvement. Why they had waited this long to question me I didn't know, but who knows how much bureaucratic paperwork they had to sort through on this case.

Regardless, Red Rain wasn't my crime. I was just a witness. Which meant I had nothing to worry about.

Feeling more confident, I replied, "What about it?"

"You were the one that discovered Dr. Nic's secret operations, were you not?" the politician asked.

"Discovered" didn't seem like an appropriate term. "Stumbled across it accidentally" would have been a more accurate description of my contribution. "I found his secret labs and was able to alert the United, yes."

"Yes, I know all about that." The man definitely smiled that time. "But while you were investigating his secret labs, what did you find out about his operation?"

"Well, I found he had forged the deaths of several scientists and was forcing them to work," I started, trying to figure out what there was to tell. Hadn't we reported this all to the United when they arrived on the scene? "And I know he had a—"

"No," the politician cut me off, "I mean, what did you find out about Red Rain? What do you know about the project itself?"

I unintentionally gaped at him. Why were they asking *me* about Red Rain? Couldn't they have found out everything they wanted from the computers—or squeezed it out of Dr. Nic himself?

A shiver passed up my spine at the thought, but even more disturbing was the fact that the United would press me for information about the project at all. What did they expect me to know?

Suddenly nothing made sense anymore.

"Were you able to find out anything about how Red Rain works?" the man pressed.

I audibly stuttered. "It... the project wasn't finished. It didn't... It doesn't work. That's why Dr. Nic requested my father, but Dad never worked on it," I added the last bit hastily, hoping I didn't just incriminate him.

"Yes, I know about your father's involvement." I didn't like how the man inflected the word "involvement." "But I'm wondering about your brother. He worked on the project the entire time he was stationed on Mars, did he not?"

"Yes, but he didn't have the knowledge to complete it. That's why—"

"I know that," the man cut me off again, and he was starting to sound somewhat annoyed. "But he worked on it a great deal and should have at least understood the theory behind it. What did he tell you about it?"

Why don't you just ask him? As much as I hated to think of Ephesus being interrogated, it would make much more sense for them to ask someone who actually worked on it than to harass me.

"Philadelphia," the man prodded me in my silence. "Tell me everything."

It was an order. The slightly benevolent tone of his voice made it even more threatening.

"He said..." I pinched my eyes shut, taking a moment to recall what Ephesus had said to me—and to pray for strength. Ephesus's exact words came back to me, and I found comfort in remembering the tone of his voice. *Philli, do you know what acid rain is?*

"Red Rain was supposed to be a concentration of chemicals that could turn normal precipitation—or even just high humidity—into an acid rain strong enough to melt metal. It was supposed to be distributed as a gas for subtlety." I took a deep breath and waited, hoping that had satisfied them.

The politician frowned at me. After a moment of silence, he seemed to pick up on the fact that I wasn't going to say any more and concluded, "That's all he told you?"

I nodded.

The man's frown deepened. "He didn't try to explain to you how it worked?" He sounded so incredulous that it made me feel stupid.

"No? I... don't really understand the technical gibberish," I managed, voice growing meek. I hunched my shoulders, wishing I could curl into a little ball to show them I was harmless. It scared me to not be able to give them what they wanted.

The politician's polished demeanor broke when he sighed and slumped back in the chair. He muttered something under his breath which I loosely translated into *"Figures."*

One of the military officers standing behind the desk spoke for the first time. "I told you she wouldn't be of any help."

I sat up straight again. That voice was familiar.

The politician's professional expression was replaced by a look of unrestrained annoyance. "All leads are worth following."

"Of course they are," the officer responded. I *did* know that voice. And it wasn't a voice I had wanted to hear ever again. "Which is why I told you she'd be very useful for other reasons."

Oh yes, it was him. I knew it before he stepped forward, bringing his face into the direct light of the desk lamp.

Former Commander Ambrose—he looked as if he had gained a few extra badges on his uniform since I last saw him—didn't greet me with anything more than a condescending smile, which was just as well. I couldn't have found the words to respond had he spoken to me.

The situation was making progressively less sense, but it was managing to get progressively more frightening.

"Watch what you say, Ambrose," the politician returned coldly. "You're on record." Somehow I got the impression that he was more worried about what I heard than what went on the recording.

Commander Ambrose smirked—a little too gleefully for my tastes—but remained silent.

The politician sighed and turned back to me. "Thank you for your cooperation," he said again, much more dryly than before. "We may have more questions for you later." He nodded at Jayde. "You may take her back."

Jayde nodded and stepped forward, but I instinctively stuck out a hand. "Wait. But why…" I faltered when I realized I didn't know quite what I was asking. I swallowed and forced myself to be pitifully blunt. "Am I still in custody?"

"Yes?" the politician replied with one raised eyebrow.

"But…" A million objections came to mind, but the politician's cold stare shot them all down before I could open my mouth. "I… I don't know anything about Red Rain. I can't help you," I managed pleadingly.

"We still may have more questions for you later," was the blanket response. "Go."

Jayde laid a hand on my arm. Desperation welled up in my head. I looked to Commander Ambrose as a last resort.

The look of bitter pleasure on his face told me everything I needed to know.

Jayde tugged on my arm. I didn't have the will to move, but I didn't have any motivation to resist, either. I allowed him to pull me to my feet and out the door.

The politician wordlessly watched me leave.

Jayde was considerate enough not to say anything as he took me back to my cell. I was in shock and walked over to sit on the cot without objection.

The beep of the door locking stirred me from my stupor. I shivered as the sense of cold aloneness overtook me again.

I didn't know what to make of this. I had done what Daddy suggested. I hadn't caused trouble. I was polite. I answered their questions. And yet that still wasn't enough.

I had been prepared for cruel opposition and harsh threats. I was ready for the United to coerce or intimidate me into fitting their mold. I had expected the officials to lay their unbending demands on me.

I was not prepared for them to have no demands at all.

5

Mrs. Nolan did come back to visit me as she'd promised. She came the next morning when Jayde brought my breakfast and promptly resumed her mothering, making sure everything in the room, myself included, was still to her satisfaction. When Jayde saw that Mrs. Nolan would be busy for a while, he left us alone, which was exactly what I'd hoped he'd do.

As soon as the door shut and I was sure Jayde was out of earshot, I asked, "Did you visit the other inmate?"

"Oh yes!" Mrs. Nolan said, not looking up from her work. She was applying some ointment to my scrape which, according to her, had scabbed "beautifully." "Not much of a talker, but she seems like a nice girl. Cute hair."

Girl? There weren't that many women left at camp. I prayed desperately it wasn't Cami.

As I suspected, Mrs. Nolan readily provided the information. "What was her name?" She crocked her head to the side. "Something short... oh yes, Cea. Unusual name, but rather sweet if you ask me. A unique name can be so attractive for a woman."

I involuntarily sucked in my breath. Mrs. Nolan looked up worriedly. "Is your leg still hurting, sweetie?"

"Oh, it just stings a little," I fudged, forcing a smile for her benefit. She returned the gesture and carried on chattering about her impression of Cea.

I wasn't listening. My mind was scrambling for clues. There had to be a reason both Cea and I were taken at the same time. One unprovoked arrest could be chalked up to the United's paranoia, but two in the same night was more than coincidental. If we had been accused of a specific crime, they surely would have told me by now. There was something else afoot, and whatever it was, somehow Cea and I were both involved.

I recalled the questions the politician had asked me yesterday. Cea had been involved in Red Rain as well, and she might even know some useful details about how it worked. But, then again, I remembered Cea telling me herself that she hated that phase of Nic's project, which is why she hadn't volunteered to help. She might not know any more than I did.

And all of this didn't explain why the United was interrogating us and not the scientists who created it.

There had to be more behind the United's motivation for arresting us, but they certainly weren't eager to give me any details. Over the course of the next three days, the politician didn't have any more questions for me. I didn't receive any contact from the officials. No word about the charges laid against me or any idea of when I'd be released. I asked if I could call home and was denied. The only visitors I received were Mrs. Nolan and routine check-ins by a guard, usually Jayde.

Mercifully, they didn't make me spend those entire three days locked in my cell with nothing to do. I'm sure I would have gone nearly insane before the end of the first day otherwise.

Jayde took me out for several hours each day. I wondered whether he had orders to do so or was simply doing it out of compassion. I didn't ask, but I was immensely grateful for the mercy.

It turned out there were several nice facilities in the building that I was allowed to use under supervision. I preferred the library best of all; even though it was all censored media, I could still amuse myself for a great while wandering the rows and hunting through the rare collection of physical books.

But even with the novelty of real paper to distract me, I quickly grew stir crazy. After three days I was not only deplorably homesick and lonely but also becoming quite worried—worried that I'd be stuck here for a very long time while the United administration crawled at its usual snail's pace. As best I could figure, I was an asset—albeit not a very useful one—to an investigation of some kind, and that meant I could be detained until the investigation was completed. Which could be indefinitely.

The thought of waiting in custody until the United managed to slog through its paperwork didn't appeal to me. I was desperate enough that, on the third day, I asked Jayde to take a message to his superiors for me. The message was either not delivered or not answered. I tried again in the morning. Still no response. By the end of the fourth day, I flat-out asked Jayde if he knew what was happening. He said no, which either meant he was just following orders in the dark, or that his orders were to keep me in the dark.

The next day, I pushed my time and wandered around the library as long as Jayde would let me. Walking peacefully back to my cell was requiring increasingly more willpower, and I wasn't sure how much more willpower I possessed.

My insistence on wandering around the library in circles proved to be providence—just as I was about to give up and go back to my cell to cry in frustration, I came around the corner to find the politician pulling a volume off the shelf.

It was definitely the same politician who had met with me the first day; even when he was casually flipping through books, he carried himself with undeniable poise. His commanding presence still frightened me, but not enough that I was deterred from walking up to him and saying, "Sir."

His controlled demeanor broke briefly as he jumped, evidently startled to find me at his elbow. His gaze quickly narrowed into a frown. "What are you doing out here?" he demanded.

Jayde was beside us in a moment. "I'm watching her, sir. I had assumed she would be allowed out of her cell for exercise."

The politician glanced at him. "Fine," he said dismissively. He snatched another book off the shelf and walked away.

"Wait!" I called. Jayde shushed me, but I ignored him and ran after the politician.

"Please, sir," I said, darting up beside him and struggling to be seen. "I just wanted to ask you if you knew when I might be able to go home."

"Not my decision," was the brisk response, and he walked faster.

I tried to keep up. "But please, sir, it's been days, and nobody's said anything to me."

"The department will let you know when we have further questions for you."

"But sir!" I cried again, not sure what else to say. "I didn't do anything!"

He didn't even respond this time.

"Miss Smyrna," Jayde said warningly from behind me.

"Please," I begged, taking one last shot. "I just want to see my father! At least let me contact—"

The politician dropped his books on the circulation desk with a startling thump. "Philadelphia," he said in his coldly calculated voice that cut off all argument, "the United has determined that you need to be in custody, and there you will remain until the officials decide otherwise." He glanced back at me. "I would also like to remind you that this is a library, and appropriate voices should be used."

Jayde grabbed my arm before I could even think of anything to say. He dragged me out of the library and hustled me down the hall. I stumbled along, the frustrated tears I had been holding abruptly revealing themselves.

"It's not fair!" I cried, my voice cracking in a sob. I sounded pathetic. Why was I complaining in front of Jayde? He wouldn't care. But then, what did it matter if he heard me? "I didn't *do* anything. I just want to go home!"

"Hey, stop it," Jayde snapped, yanking on my arm.

I winced. Guess I was wrong. He *did* care. I snapped my mouth shut and did my best to dam another sob.

"I said stop!" he yelled again, this time shoving me roughly.

"Jayde!" I cried, annoyed. I wasn't doing anything!

"That's *enough*!" And faster than I could blink, he had me slammed against the wall, pinning me down with his arm.

"Don't you ever try that again," he snarled.

My heart was beating so fast I couldn't respond. What had I done? Jayde's face was so close to mine I was afraid to even draw a breath.

And then I realized that this position also allowed Jayde to put his mouth discretely close to my ear.

"This is off the record," he said, suddenly talking in a nearly unintelligible whisper. "But you're not here because of anything you've done."

I swallowed and waited.

"You and that other girl are here because of a project they want some scientists to work on."

What scientists? Even as the thought passed across my consciousness, I felt stupid for missing the obvious. They wanted my father and brother, of course.

"I don't know what the project is, but they've taken the scientists to a lab across town, and—"

"Is this young man harassing you, Philli?"

Both Jayde and I jumped and turned to see Commander Ambrose approaching us at a stroll. The sight of his cruel expression made me remember what he had said that first day. *Which is why I told you she'd be very useful for other reasons.*

Suddenly everything made sense. True, hard, brutal sense.

Looking at the rich anticipation in Ambrose's eyes, I briefly wondered if I would have rather stayed in blissful ignorance.

"Everything's under control, sir," Jayde said in a voice that was entirely unphased.

"Oh, I wasn't worried about you," Commander Ambrose crowed benevolently. "I have no doubt that a strong man like you could handle her."

Both Jayde and I were equally put out by that statement.

"I'm more worried about her causing trouble. She's a stubborn one." He actually had the audacity to wink at me.

It took all my willpower not to make a sassy face at him. I had to keep up the act.

Turning to Jayde, I said very meekly, "It won't happen again, sir."

He nodded briskly. "Good. Come along." He grabbed my arm and guided me down the hall, giving Commander Ambrose a respectful nod as he passed.

I couldn't resist a stolen glance back at Ambrose. He was grinning.

Jayde didn't talk as he led me back to my room, which was just as well. My mind was spinning, rapidly snapping the pieces together.

We were hostages, Cea and I. A bargaining chip to force my father and brother to comply with the United's wishes. I couldn't guess what the United wanted them for, but if the United felt the need to use hostages to intimidate them into complying, it must be serious. And more than likely it was something immoral, unethical, and dangerous.

But if they wanted to coerce my father and brother, why did they need Cea? Was there really more going on between Ephesus and Cea than I realized? How had the United found out?

Unanswered questions still burned in the back of my mind, but I shoved them aside. Only one thing was important right now.

I had to talk to Cea. And I knew who could help arrange a meeting.

6

As usual, Mrs. Nolan visited me during breakfast the next morning.

"Looks like you're healing well," she said with proud satisfaction. "Just don't pick at the scab."

I slowly laid the groundwork for my proposition. "How is Cea doing?"

Mrs. Nolan scrunched her nose in concerned thought. "Better. She had a few nasty scrapes and bruises when she came in, but I think she's feeling mostly herself again."

I poked at my breakfast, as if that reinforced my casualness. "Yeah... she must be feeling pretty lonely, though."

"Oh, no doubt, poor thing!" Mrs. Nolan fussed as she remade my bed for the second time.

"I mean, being in prison, and hurt, without any family or friends to visit you..."

Mrs. Nolan made a *tsk, tsk* noise as she bustled about the room doing her routine maintenance.

"I mean, it's been bad enough for me, and I'm not hurt..."

"I know, sweetheart."

She still didn't pick up on it. I decided to be blunt. "I guess… I would just really like to visit her."

Mrs. Nolan stopped. I held my breath, praying, and waited to see how she would take it.

"You know what," she declared after a moment, "a visit is just what you two need!"

Hope surged through my veins. *Yes, thank you!*

"I'll make it happen. Doctor's orders." She smiled. I returned the gesture.

Mrs. Nolan's influence worked wonders yet again—although I wouldn't have been surprised if Jayde had a hand in it as well—and at lunchtime she came to get me. She took me up a floor to a place where the hallway bowed out in a little glass-walled sitting area. A few tables and chairs were scattered around, and one was topped with a dainty little lunch for two.

I guess Mrs. Nolan took the whole "visit" idea seriously.

I thanked her profusely for more reasons than one and sat down to wait. Within a few minutes Cea came up, escorted by Jayde. I was glad it was him; at least I could trust him to keep his distance.

Sure enough, he led Cea to the table and then walked across the hall to the nearest bench—far enough away that he couldn't hear us if we talked softly.

I wasn't really interested in eating, but I knew it would look suspicious if I didn't touch my food. I said grace, using the time to pray for guidance, and took a bite before starting.

Cea stared at me until I looked up, then said with loaded casualness, "That nurse seems to like you."

"She's nice," I replied with a shrug. "He's friendly, too." I gestured with my shoulder at Jayde.

Cea glanced at him, then turned her attention back to me. "Does he talk to you at all? My guard won't even say hello."

After throwing a look around the hall to make sure we were alone, I forewent the cryptic talk and lowered my voice to a whisper. "He said it's not because of anything we've done."

"Figured that much out myself," Cea replied dryly.

"He said it's because the United wants to make some scientists work on a project. I assume he means my father and brother."

"Ephesus," she breathed, and there was more than one emotion attached to the name.

I took the handy opportunity to voice my suspicions. "But if it's my family they want, I don't know why they need you."

Somewhat to my disappointment, Cea did not divulge her affections. She furrowed her brow for an awkwardly long moment, long enough for inspiration to hit her. She jerked her head up, eyes wide like she'd been punched. "Nic. They've got Nic."

It was my turn to stare in uncomfortable silence. Suddenly Dr. Nic's apparent disappearance from the records made sense. The United had kept him and his unlawful genius to themselves.

Cea's gears were still churning. "But what…" She trailed off and nibbled on her sandwich. I copied her and pretended to eat.

She set her sandwich down and looked back up at me. "Did the rich guy meet with you too?"

I nodded, trying to chew my mouthful quickly.

"What did he ask you about?"

I swallowed a bite of fruit. "Red Rain…" I started to say.

I almost didn't get all the way through the name. Hearing it out loud, suddenly I understood. I knew what was going on.

The look on Cea's face confirmed it.

"But why?" I gasped, mostly because I hoped it wasn't true.

"Why not?" she returned. "Why wouldn't a tyrannical government want a weapon that could desecrate its resistance?"

That's why there was no mention of Dr. Nic or his project in the news. The United wanted Red Rain for themselves.

And they were going to force my father and brother to help Dr. Nic create it.

Dear God, no.

"We have to get out of here," Cea hissed.

"What?" I said loudly, still not thinking clearly.

Cea cast a nervous look at Jayde. He glanced up at us briefly but then returned his attention to his handheld device.

Cea leaned in closer. "We can't let them use us as hostages. We have to escape before they can pull that card."

Escape? The word made my chest instantly cramp in dread. How did she expect us to break out of here? By beating up the guards?

No, there had to be a better way. "It won't work," I said confidently. "My father won't work on the project, no matter what."

"The fewer bargaining chips the United has, the better. I'm not taking chances with this," she returned. "We're getting out of here as soon as we can."

"But—" I started, my mind racing through a million objections and concerns.

"Phil." Cea reached out and touched my hand. "Trust me. I know what we're dealing with, and I know that we can't let the United have Red Rain. Think about what they would do with it."

I didn't need to think about it. They would do what Dr. Nic had been planning to do with it, only they wouldn't show any discretion about who they bombed. Dr. Nic had intended to use Red Rain to defend his haven; the United would use it to destroy all havens.

Cea squeezed my hand. "I'll make the call as soon as I can."

"Call?" I questioned.

"I've got a phone I can use to call some friends." She said it with absolutely no regard for how phenomenal a feat that was. "But I'll only be able to use it once before the United recognizes the device, so we'll have to time it right. Do you think that nurse would arrange another lunch if you asked her?"

"Yes," I said. My mind was spinning over everything, but Mrs. Nolan's affection for me was one thing I could be confident of.

"Okay," Cea said, sounding encouraged. "I'll let you know by sending a message through her."

I closed my eyes and took a deep breath, trying to muster a comparable amount of courage. *It will be all right. With Mrs. Nolan's cooperation, we can get out of our cells. Then we just need to distract Jayde and slip out a back door. You can do this.*

"I need you to take this."

I looked up to see Cea slowly unzipping her jacket. A small pistol was tucked into her belt.

I couldn't bite back a gasp.

"You'll need it." She carefully slipped the pistol out and held it down out of sight below the table.

"How did you even get that in here?" I squeaked.

She looked up into my face. "It's not metal. Besides, I gave the guards something else to think about on the way in."

I frowned at her. Looking closely, I could see the ghosts of healing cuts and bruises on her face and arms, and I remembered what Mrs. Nolan had said. My eyes widened.

"Here." She extended her hand beneath the table. "It's loaded. I've got one for myself, and between us that should be enough bullets."

I didn't make a move to take it. "Enough bullets for what?" I said, even though I genuinely didn't want the answer.

"Enough to get us out of here."

I stared at her. Did she want us to shoot our way out of here like terrorists? I couldn't. I *wouldn't.* My father would never approve.

"I-I don't know how to shoot," I fudged, even though that wasn't entirely true. I remembered learning gun safety with Grandpa as a child. But that was before the United started using guns to keep us in concentration camps.

"It's easy," she said callously. "Just press the red button on the back to turn it on. It does everything else automatically; you just have to pull the trigger."

She tapped me on the knee with the hilt. I squirmed back. She frowned at me impatiently. "Hurry, take it before someone sees!"

I instinctively threw a glance at Jayde. At that exact moment, he looked up at me.

He didn't even lift his head; he just shifted slightly and caught my gaze out of the corner of his eye.

We looked at each other for a split second. A split second in which he had the opportunity to turn away and pretend he never saw anything.

He didn't take it.

"Hey, drop that gun!" he ordered, rising.

Cea didn't obey. Instead she stood up, switched the pistol on, and fired.

I screamed. Thankfully she missed Jayde, instead puncturing the wall behind him. Jayde threw us one scowling look before taking off at a run.

"Guess I'm making that call now." With a furious look, she turned and forced the gun into my hands. "Now you've got one less bullet. Pay attention!"

I held the weapon away from me. "But I—"

"Just do as I say and we'll make it out of here! Come on!" She took off in the direction Jayde went.

I didn't have any choice but to follow. I wasn't about to stand there and get caught with a gun in my hands.

I ran after her, struggling not to fall behind. "But the elevator is back the other way!"

"Exactly! This way!" She turned around a corner.

I followed her as she twisted through random side halls, ending up in a deserted corner by a janitorial storage room. She halted just outside the door to the stairwell.

"They'll be expecting us to head straight for the doors. If we throw them off it will give us a minute's headway." She reached down and slid a cellphone out of her shoe as she talked. It was dated slim touchscreen, one of those smartphones from the 2020s. She slid her fingers across the screen and dialed.

I wondered if the thing would even work. But after only a brief pause, the call connected.

"Hi," Cea said. "I'd like to order pizza to be delivered."

It took my mind a moment to even process what she was saying. *Did she just…?*

"Yes. Two medium house specialties, please. With drinks."

She did. "Cea—"

She shushed me harshly. "Yes. That's for Caesar. Deliver to 1217 North 13th Street, please. Thank you."

She hung up. I suddenly had significantly less hope in our escape.

"What in the world was that?" I screeched, trying not to panic and failing significantly.

"Just trust me." She switched the cellphone for her other pistol and turned it on. I remembered I was holding a gun and hastily slipped it into the pocket of my jacket. Hopefully I wouldn't accidentally shoot myself or something.

She walked up to the stairwell door and peered through the window. "Coast clear, at least on this floor. Now, listen. We have to go quietly and not too fast. That way, if someone on another floor happens to see us, we won't look immediately suspicious."

She pushed the door open slowly and stepped through. I followed, wondering if the rapid beating of my heart was enough to make someone suspicious.

We started down the stairs. I focused on watching where I put my feet, struggling not to trip or make too much noise. *Just keep moving. All the way to the bottom. Don't panic. You can slip out the back way and everything will be—*

"They're down here!"

Oh dear God.

Cea had already broken into a run and was nearly half a floor ahead of me. "They're several floors back! We can make it ahead of them!"

I grabbed the railing and ran, but my feet suddenly seemed to want to tangle with each other. I couldn't move fast enough. Cea slipped further ahead while the shouts behind me grew closer. "Stop! Stop right there!"

A little voice inside me echoed them. *Stop. Just stop right here and sit. They won't hurt you if you don't fight back.*

Cea paused at the foot of the stairs to wait for me to catch up. "Come *on*, Phil!"

I jumped two steps to the last landing. I glanced at the door just in time to see a guard approaching from the hall. He was nearly at the door. "Cea, there's more in the hall!"

"Shoot the door panel!" she yelled.

"What?" I shouted back.

She didn't wait for me to figure it out. She took aim from where she was and shot at the security panel by the door. I screamed and instinctively dropped to the floor as pieces of glass flew. Cea fired three more times, shredding the inner electronics.

I shielded my face with a shriek as sparks and smoke spewed from the panel. Cea's voice cut through the ringing in my ears. "Keep going, Phil!"

I stumbled to my feet, coughing and trying to fan the smoke out of my face. I heard cursing from the other side of the door, and then something banged against it. Once, twice, three times, and then the door groaned open, revealing a guard with his gun pointed at me.

Before I could react, a shot fired from below. The guard slumped over and hit the ground with a thud, almost before the moan escaped his mouth.

I grabbed my throat as I watched in mesmerized horror. *He's... he's... she didn't!*

"Philli, *now!*"

I gagged. Lurching forward, I stumbled down the last flight of stairs and nearly fell into Cea.

"Cea, that guard back there, he's..."

She wasn't even listening. She fired several more times back in the direction I had come from. I slapped my hands over my ears as I heard several more guards meet their demise.

Without a word Cea grabbed my arm and yanked me through the door to the parking ramp. Kicking the door shut, she blasted that security panel to pieces too.

"That should slow them." Her gun clicked dully. "I'm out. Where's your gun?"

I just shook my head rapidly, my hands still over my ears.

"Phil, stop it. Come on." She took off at a run again.

I looked up to see where she was going. For a brief moment, hope fluttered through my shaky heart. The parking garage seemed deserted.

Please, God, no more guards. No more shooting.

But then I saw them—guards coming down the stairs at the opposite end of the lot.

Before I could get the words out to warn Cea, one of the guards yelled, and the place erupted in shouts and barked orders. More guards poured down the stairwell and surged towards us, weaving between the parked vehicles like an army of rats.

I stared at the approaching danger, at first too disheartened to even process the situation. Distant yelling from behind reminded me that going back was not an option. *Dead end.*

Cea froze, then spun around to face me. "Philli!" she yelled. "Your gun!"

I jerked out of my stupor. I hastily pulled the lethal weapon out of my pocket and fiddled with the button. The gun hummed to life, vibrating in my hands. I fitted it in my palm and put my feet apart, just like Grandpa had taught me. And then I looked up at the army of approaching guards.

I stopped. What was I doing?

"Come on, Phil!"

Did she expect me to blast through them? Did she expect me to kill?

"Shoot!" she shrieked.

She did. She expected me to gun them down, one by one, cutting through them like underbrush blocking the path.

"Shoot, Philli, now!" she continued to holler, panic making her voice nearly unintelligible. *"Shoot!"*

I focused my eyes on the nearest guard. His iron-gray hair betrayed his age. He looked about as old as my father.

Daddy...

I let the gun slip from my hands. I heard it bounce on the floor.

Cea continued to shriek at me. I wasn't listening. I sagged against the nearest support beam, suddenly aware of my exhaustion. The will to stand left me as the adrenaline drained from my nerves.

Cea dove for the gun, but the first guard reached us at the same moment. He lurched forward and kicked Cea squarely under the chin. She dropped to the ground with a cry, blood splattering from her lips.

I screamed, a new kind of panic surging through me. "No, please don't hurt—"

I didn't get to finish my plea. Someone grabbed me and cuffed my hands behind my back in one swift motion. Before I could even turn my head, they spun me around and shoved me into someone who gripped me with powerful hands.

I looked up to see a captain of some sort glaring down at me. "What is the meaning of this?" he snarled, punctuating the threat by giving me a hard shake.

I wasn't sure he actually expected an answer to that question, but I knew I couldn't come up with a sensible one. I stared at him, blood pounding in my ears.

"Captain!" My heart plummeted at the sound of the familiar voice. It was Jayde.

He didn't even look at me. "The commander wants them transferred to headquarters immediately for questioning and punishment." He held out a communicator with a message displayed on the screen as proof.

I didn't even try to read what it said. The word "punishment" swirled around in my head, crowding out all other thoughts with dark fear.

The captain drew his eyebrows together in a scowl. "Blindfold them," he snapped, shoving me towards Jayde.

This time Jayde did not object.

He did as he was told, dragged me a few steps to the right, and then threw me like unwanted luggage. I hit the floor of a vehicle hard. Blotches of color flashed across the darkness in front of my face. I heard Cea hit the ground beside me with a grunt. What sounded like van doors slammed behind us.

Heated talking continued outside the van for a moment, which was silenced by a harsh order. The vehicle rocked as the cabin doors slammed, and then the engine roared to life. The heavy vibration ground right beneath my head, giving me a debilitating headache on top of everything else.

The van surged forward roughly, sending me skidding to the side. I tried to hold steady until the van dipped up the exit ramp and turned, where the driving leveled out. Then I collapsed on the ground, letting my every joint go limp.

Cea groaned. "Philli?" she mumbled, so hoarsely that I wasn't sure she was really talking to me. Either way, I didn't answer. I didn't want to talk.

Another groan and some shuffling. It sounded like she was trying to sit up. "Philli?" she said again, more clearly. "It will be all right."

For an answer, I turned my face to the wall and sobbed.

I didn't care what she thought, or if the guards heard me. I didn't care about facing my punishment bravely, not when I'd brought it on myself.

There had been no reason to cause trouble; no one was getting hurt. If we had complied, waited quietly in special custody until the United realized bargaining wouldn't work, we all would have survived. But now several guards were injured, probably dead, and we were going to be punished. We had gained nothing—only caused more pain.

My father would be horrified when he found out.

If he ever found out. My chances of being returned home to him were slim now, and I knew it. If I had just waited out my confinement quietly, they probably would have sent me home. Now I'd be lucky if they just stuck me in a higher-security prison.

And what would become of my father? How would our stunt affect him and Ephesus? Would they be in trouble because the hostages had tried to escape? What would the United do to them now?

I couldn't bear to think of the possibilities. I couldn't bear to think that I had caused my father pain.

Please, God, I begged, even though I felt like I didn't deserve to ask anything of Him. *Don't let them—*

The van lurched around a corner, throwing me into the wall. The resulting pain was an almost welcome diversion. Before I even had time to regain my bearings, the van swerved again, dealing me another blow. This time, darkness mercifully washed over my mind, and I knew nothing more.

7

I woke up to darkness. It took me only a fraction of a second to realize it was dark because I was still blindfolded.

I lay still, letting the unwanted memory flow back to me. With it came an ache in nearly every joint and bone—and the realization that I was no longer handcuffed.

I stiffened, involuntarily clenching my hands into fists. Why would they let me go? I must be in a secured room. Had they locked me alone in a cell to await my punishment?

I couldn't think of anything more horrible.

But at least I didn't have to wait in the dark. If they'd removed the handcuffs, they obviously couldn't stop me from taking the blindfold off.

I sat up gingerly, groaning a little under my breath as dizziness and pain assaulted me. I waited for my head to clear, then reached up and felt for the knot in the cloth.

A voice called out, making me suddenly realize I wasn't alone.

"You might not want to do that just yet."

I stopped, but not because of the admonition. I knew that voice. And it wasn't Cea's.

"Don't torment her. The United did enough of that." *That* was Cea.

"I just don't want to startle her," the other person said again. His voice sounded exactly like I remembered it—cool and even, almost disinterested, forcibly propped up with a hint of arrogance. But it couldn't be him. Why would he be here?

"As if waking up blindfolded isn't startling enough," Cea returned.

"Probably less startling than waking up and seeing me," he replied without any sarcasm. I had to admit that he was right, but my shock was quickly giving way to hope—hope that he might still be a friend.

I yanked the blindfold off and gasped out his name in the same breath. "Stanyard."

He sat across from me with his arms folded on his knees. Wherever we were was dark, with only one electric lantern illuminating the room, but there was enough light for me to make out his features. He hadn't changed one bit; he even wore the same calm, slightly moody stare.

I wondered if that meant his opinions hadn't changed, either.

Questions welled up inside me, but none seemed as important as: "What are you doing here?"

"Glad to see me, huh?" he returned, his subtle, wry smile showing itself. Cea, who was sitting nearby, chuckled. I flushed, realizing that hadn't been a very friendly greeting.

"I'm saving your skin, that's what," he declared, leaning his chin on his arms.

That statement made me pause to take in my surroundings. I quickly realized we weren't in a prison or a government building of any kind. It looked like we were in a cellar—stained concrete walls, crates and junk scattered around, and a damp, musty smell hanging in the air.

"Welcome to my basement," Stanyard said without ceremony, confirming my suspicions.

I turned back to him. "But how—"

"You have Jayde to thank," he answered my unfinished question. "I just took you in and stashed you out of sight."

"Jayde?" I exclaimed. "But he..." I couldn't bring myself to say it out loud. *He betrayed me. But was it really betrayal? He was just doing his job. He's a government agent, not my friend.*

"That's what it's supposed to look like," Stanyard said, as if reading my thoughts. "That order to take you to headquarters for punishment? It was fake."

Cea grinned deviously, confirming his statement.

My eyes widened in a combination of amazement and alarm. "Will he be blamed if they find out?"

"Not if he's smart and does his job right," Stanyard retorted. "If he follows the steps, it will look on paper as though your van was hijacked by rebels, and the fake order will be attributed to someone hacking the system from the outside."

I didn't know what to say. I didn't even know how to swallow it all. "So he's... you're..." I groped, begging for an explanation.

"Yup. We're both members of the underground. Augustine at your service." Stanyard extended his hand jauntily.

"And I'm Caesar," Cea chirped.

I gaped at her. *Augustine? Caesar?* Who makes up names like that? "That... doesn't sound anything like you," I managed.

"That's the point of code names," Stanyard quipped.

I glared at him. They were starting to sound like little kids playing superheroes. Was he even being serious?

"What?" he returned in response to my look. "Do you expect us to go around using our real names? You know as well as I do that the United listens to everything."

Suddenly everything began to make at least some sense in my head. I glanced at Cea. "So when you made that call..."

"Yes, I was passing a call for help to the underground."

"Underground?" I repeated.

"What else would you call it?" Stanyard said. "It's not exactly formal. It's just a network of communication amongst people who are willing to help."

"Are they all Christians?" I asked, struggling to put the last pieces of the puzzle together.

"No. Some are just citizens who are fed up with the United. Like Jayde." Stanyard paused, his voice sobering suddenly. "And me."

I saw that as an opportunity to broach the more personal questions burning in my heart. "So you're still legally part of the Outside?"

"Technically," he replied without enthusiasm. "My standing is hanging by a thread, but I've managed to hold onto my job."

"Job?" I asked out of pure curiosity.

"Pizza delivery," he explained, smiling somewhat. "My 'day job' is running a little pizza shop above ground."

"So that's why Cea ordered pizza," I declared.

Cea winked. "Best deep-crust in town."

Stanyard laughed. "Yes. Running the shop feeds me and also keeps the United off my tail. As long as the shop appears to be following regulations on paper, they don't snoop into what I'm really doing with my business. This is the second-level basement under the shop. On their map, the building only has one basement, where I live."

I could only nod in wonder. I wasn't sure what to say, but I wanted to hear more. I wanted to hear everything. "What's it like?"

"What, sleeping in a basement?" he replied, his dry smirk returning.

"No… Living. In the Outside."

He finally locked eyes with me. After sharing a long stare, he admitted in a husky voice, "Horrible."

"What? Really?" I exclaimed.

Stanyard shushed me harshly. Snapping my mouth shut, I inwardly scolded myself for being so surprised. It was the Outside, ruled by godless people who wanted all citizens to deny their religion. Of course it would be horrible to live there. That's what we had been raised to believe, told to repeat in our minds to keep ourselves from temptation. You didn't want to join the Outside. No one did.

And yet, I knew that none of us, even the adults, truly believed that. We all believed—hoped, perhaps—that the Outside was something better. That there was more to life beyond the walls of the concentration camps. That out there, somewhere, existed freedom.

Stanyard glanced around the basement, dark eyes flashing with worry. "Keep it down," he hissed, voice a whisper for emphasis. "This basement doesn't exist, remember. I've got the TV on loud in my room, but you can't take chances."

I bit my tongue, suddenly afraid to make any sound, and waited for more explanation.

When he turned back to me, his expression was filled with an emotion I hadn't seen from him in a long time—fear. "You can't breathe out here. There's too many ways to make a mistake and arouse their suspicion."

"All the regulations?" I ventured in a suitably quiet voice.

He gave a little snort. "They don't even follow their own standards. It's whatever pleases them at any given moment. If it makes a government official or your neighbor worry, it's against the law, and you're out."

"Your neighbor?" I frowned.

"Backbiters," he said, voice heavy. "I've never seen a culture so self-centered. The government isn't actually as omnipresent as some make it out to be. They have access to all your data, but they don't have time to monitor it. But the people you pass on the street... They can report you at any time. And they will. Some do it to keep from being accused of harboring you should you turn out to be doing something illegal. Others do it to get on an official's good side, or to keep the United off of their own tail. Even members of the underground do it to each other to shift the blame. I've had to fend off the United's dogs a few times myself."

"That's the main reason Nic settled on Mars. Things are a lot less tedious when your nearest neighbor is twenty miles away and has to don a spacesuit to come spy on you," Cea contributed.

Stanyard sighed and leaned his chin on his arms again. "I don't mind playing mind games with the government," he said candidly, "but I hate having to treat everyone around me like a traitor. You can't trust anyone."

You can trust me, I wanted to say, but didn't.

"Trouble is," Stanyard continued, leaning back against the wall, "the United doesn't exactly ask for proof of wrongdoing before locking you up. I've done some time in 'special custody' waiting for stuff to blow over."

"Tell us about it," Cea groused.

"How have you managed this long?" I asked with more than a small amount of admiration.

He shrugged. "You learn the tricks of staying low. Everyone else, even the officials, are just trying to get by. If you make their lives easier by doing what's expected of you and not getting in their way, they'll leave you alone. You become part of the scenery. Play the part of a well-oiled gear and the system won't kick you out."

"Just play by the rules," I muttered, to which he nodded. *Just like life in the camp*, I thought, the realization settling in. The game truly was the same, assimilated or not. Play by the rules and nobody gets hurt.

"Well, I need to be getting back," Stanyard said suddenly. His voice was falsely cheerful, which I knew was his way of ending the conversation. "Can't stay away too long, or someone might worry."

He stood up and walked past me. I turned to see a ladder bolted to the wall. "Do you think they're watching you in your room?" I stood up to follow him but nearly fell back down when I realized how stiff my legs were. I ungracefully braced myself against the wall.

He glanced over his shoulder. "Not directly. But I can't take chances. One careless step could put us all in danger."

I nodded numbly, suddenly burdened by all the risks he was taking to hide us after we'd been dumped on his doorstep without warning. "Thank you," I said, hoping he understood.

He nodded and grabbed the ladder, stepping up on the first rung.

"Wait!" I cried, suddenly finding the courage to ask the question I had been holding back. I dreaded the answer, but I wanted to hear it from him. "Where's Mira?"

He stared at me. The sadness in his expression clearly answered my question.

He stepped back off the ladder. "She left," he related in a quiet tone. "Ran away from our host family and married a soldier before she was even of legal age. She hasn't written me in months. I'm not sure where she is."

I involuntarily clenched my skirt in my fingers. Wailing questions swirled through my head, fueled by pain and betrayal. *Why would she do that? How could she leave her own brother?* Looking into Stanyard's face, I knew he had spent many long nights torturing himself with the same unanswerable questions.

"Why did you never write me?" I asked abruptly. "I mean us. Back at camp."

"I couldn't," he said with a careless shrug. "Former unassimilated can't contact those that are still noncompliant. Even the underground couldn't get my emails through. Once you leave, you can't even speak of those left behind. The United acts as if the camps and their inhabitants don't exist. I guess it's part of their policy to keep us from going back."

"Why didn't you come back?" The painful question slipped off my tongue before I could stop it.

His eyes darkened defensively. I expected him to snap at me, but he didn't. What he did say was worse.

"Come back to what?" His voice was cold and utterly dry.

Come back home. To your father. To your friends. To God. To me. So many responses swirled around in my head, but I couldn't find the courage to say any of them. This time, I was the one who looked away.

I heard Stanyard climbing the ladder. "I'll be back in the morning," he said in his normal tone. "Stay down here and remember to be quiet."

I glanced up in time to see him disappear through the hole in the ceiling. The door closed after him, and there was the sound of something heavy being dragged on top. I felt like something heavy had been dropped on my heart, too.

"I wish we were back on Mars," Cea suddenly declared, thankfully disturbing my thoughts.

"Yeah," was all I could say, thinking of my brief visit to the base. If it weren't for Dr. Nic's obsession with apocalyptic weapons, it would have been wonderful. No one had been afraid to breathe up there, even us unassimilated. We had all wanted to stay.

But I was a fool for thinking the rest of the Outside was like that. The only reason Dr. Nic had been able to build his own little kingdom without United interference was because the base had been so remote.

I jolted out of my moody daze when I remembered what else was at stake. I turned to Cea. "What about my family, and Nic? Are they going to be... all right?" There was more I wanted to ask—namely, *"Will we ever see them again?"*—but I couldn't bring myself to phrase it so bluntly.

She gazed at me. I recognized her expression as the look of an adult who's struggling to decide how honest to be with a child. "We'll just have to trust Augustine and the others," she settled for finally.

"But what can they do about it? Are they going to—"

"Just wait and see," she said firmly, making it very clear that she didn't want to say any more. "You need to rest."'

I indulged in a childish pout. "I just woke up."

Her lips twitched with amused affection. "Being knocked cold doesn't count as sleeping. Lie down and try to rest." She gestured over to the corner, where a few blankets and pillows were stacked.

I relinquished with a sigh and did as I was told, curling up against the wall between some crates. Having boxes around me made me feel safer and less cold.

Before long, Cea dimmed the electric lantern and laid down on her own makeshift bed. I assumed she fell asleep because of the thick silence that settled soon after.

Still wide awake, I listened hard into the darkness, trying to grasp any sound from above. Nothing. Of course Stanyard had probably fallen asleep, but it would have given me great comfort to hear his footsteps on the floor, to know that there was someone out there. To know that we weren't completely alone, shut in a dark basement like fugitive criminals.

I shivered. We *were* fugitive criminals. Even if the United believed the van hijacking story, they would know we were still on the run. Whether or not they would bother searching for us I couldn't guess. Maybe we weren't worth it. But we would still be wanted, and we couldn't show our faces above ground without risking getting caught. We couldn't even turn ourselves in at the camp; Commander Clint would know what we had done.

My throat and chest tightened at the realization. We couldn't go home. Not ever.

Clutching the blanket in my stiff fingers, I sobbed into the darkness.

8

I didn't sleep all night. Therefore, I was wide awake when muffled voices broke the silence several hours later.

After my brain roused enough to process that noise was coming from the room above and that there was more than one voice talking, I realized I should be worried. Only Stanyard was supposed to be up there. Who else could there be?

I was too groggy to process the terrible possibilities, much less do anything about them, so I sat with my arms around my knees and listened while the heavy object over the hatch was dragged away. They hadn't even opened the door all the way before I could hear the voices clearly enough to identify them. All my worry vanished, along with the remembrance that I was supposed to keep my voice down.

"Daddy!" I shrieked, scrambling up so fast I tripped.

Stanyard shushed me from above, but I willfully ignored him. All my attention was focused on the familiar pair of Oxford shoes and long white lab coat descending the ladder. I darted over and grabbed him around the waist before he had even stepped off the last rung.

The man didn't return my hug. "Glad to see me, Philadelphia? I wish I could say the same of you."

I gave a muted squeal of terror and jerked back. Stanyard shushed me again, and this time I was too stunned to make another sound. I looked up into the stoic face of Dr. Nic, half-expecting him to fly into a rage.

Thankfully, Cea spared me further embarrassment by grasping her brother in a hug and pulling him away. My dad was the next one down the ladder.

"Philli," he said, expressing all his emotion in that loving name.

"Daddy," I said, much more quietly, but no less joyfully. I threw myself into his arms, fighting the sudden urge to cry.

"Oh Philli, I'm so glad to see you." He smoothed his hands over my hair and kissed my head, then held me away from him. "Are you all right?"

"I... I think so," I managed, the events of the past few days suddenly swirling through my head. Now I would have to tell him what I'd done.

"What happened?" Ephesus joined us and scrutinized me with a frown. "Did you not sleep at all?"

I flushed a little. My face must look terrible. "No... I got knocked out on the way in, and now I'm not tired, I guess."

My father sucked in his breath sharply. Dr. Nic piped up helpfully from across the room. "You know they used to say that sleeping after a concussion can kill you."

I gaped at him in horror. Was he serious? What if I had—

"Leave her alone," Ephesus snapped.

"It's just an urban legend," Nic returned. "No medical truth to it."

Ephesus ignored him. He laid a hand on both Daddy and me. "Come on, let's talk over here."

Daddy guided me over to the corner, and we all sat down in a circle. Ephesus gave my shoulder a squeeze, and then Daddy took both of my hands in his.

"Now, tell me what happened."

I took a deep breath and obeyed. I told him everything, every detail. I watched his expression as I talked. He didn't interrupt, only rubbed my hands encouragingly, but I could see the emotions flickering across his eyes—slowly, like a lagging video feed. And they were exactly what I had expected to see: worry, fear, shock, then grief. Finally, disappointment.

I finished with a sigh. "I'm sorry, Daddy."

"Don't be sorry," Ephesus said quickly. "You did what you had to. I'm proud of you two." He touched my arm.

I glanced at Daddy. He didn't look proud, but he didn't scold me, either. "I'm sorry we put you through that," he said with a sigh.

"It's not your fault," I said, almost indignantly.

He smiled, a strangely sad sort of smile that I wasn't sure how to interpret. "Never mind," he said, patting my hand. "It's over now."

I realized they hadn't told me their side of the story. "How did you get here?"

"We broke out and Augustine picked us up," Ephesus answered.

"How did you break out? Break out from where?" I asked slowly, wondering if I even wanted to know.

Ephesus smirked triumphantly. "Just some secured lab across town. Some computer hacking did wonders on the security systems."

"Yeah, and your bombs helped too," Dr. Nic chirped. Clearly he was listening to our conversation.

"Bombs?" I squeaked, and then suddenly had the feeling that we'd had this conversation before. "The same bombs you were—"

"Yes," Ephesus replied, voice sour with a grudge. "Apparently the United salvaged all my work from Mars and gave it to Dr. Nic to play with."

"Well, it turned out to be useful, didn't it?" Dr. Nic returned. "We'd have never made it out of there otherwise."

Guns. Bombs. And not just any bombs. The horrendously destructive bombs Dr. Nic had been creating to threaten Earth. And now the United had it all.

"Never mind," my father said again, more sternly this time. "It's over."

"Dad," Ephesus protested. "She deserves to know."

"I don't want to talk about it," Daddy outright snapped. Then he sighed, as if he realized how prickly his voice sounded. "What's done is done, but it's behind us now. The important part is that we all made it out alive, and we're together."

"You're right," Ephesus said with a little sigh of his own. "I'm sorry. I'm glad you're safe, Phil. Come here." He opened his arms for a hug.

I accepted it and squeezed him around the neck. After a moment, I whispered, "It didn't work, did it?"

"What?" Ephesus asked, setting me away from him.

"The United keeping us as hostages. Did they threaten you with us?"

Ephesus glanced at Daddy. I followed his gaze. "Yes, they told us that's why they had you in custody. I suspect that's why they arrested you before bringing us to the lab," Daddy said.

"What did they say they'd do to us?" I asked, feeling morbidly curious.

Daddy shook his head, his eyes suddenly looking everywhere but into my own. "They wouldn't say. Just that there would be trouble if we didn't make progress."

"What did you do?" I slid back over to him and found his hand, eager to hear his side of the tale.

Daddy didn't answer for a long moment. Ephesus spoke first. "*I* worked on hacking the computer and finding an escape route."

I looked up at him with a frown, disturbed by the sharpness of his voice. He was scowling furiously at our father.

I turned to Dad, worry rising in my chest. "Daddy, what happened?"

Daddy squeezed my hand. "I did work on it a little."

"A little?" Dr. Nic objected. "Old man, you nearly had it!"

"Shut *up*," Ephesus snapped, and he sounded like he meant it.

My heart was in my throat. "Daddy, you *worked* on it?"

He finally met my gaze. "It was the only way. If they didn't see progress, there would have been trouble for all of us."

The only way? The only option was to surrender and give the United a lethal weapon?

"I didn't finish it," Daddy continued. "We couldn't make it work. I highly doubt it will ever be operational."

That was good news. It should comfort me to know that the United still didn't have Red Rain.

But somehow it didn't make me feel any better.

"It did buy us enough time to escape," Ephesus inserted, trying to sound encouraging. "Now their game's up."

And the United had won. Their bargaining chip had worked.

"They won't get Red Rain from us now. Will they?" Ephesus gripped Daddy's shoulder.

Daddy laid his hand on top of Ephesus's and looked into his son's face. "No. It's over, and we're all safe. There's nothing else they can do to us now."

Safe for how long? We were all fugitives. We would always be fugitives.

Daddy squeezed my hand again, distracting me. "I brought something for you." He retracted his hand to reach into his coat pocket.

I looked up to see him pull out my reader. Sudden joy shoved all other thoughts aside. "But how did you..."

"I brought it with me when they took us to the lab." He laid it in my lap.

I untangled the power cord and clasped the device in my hands, savoring the familiar feel of the buttons.

"I kept it with me because I knew I'd find you eventually, and I wanted to be able to give it to you." Daddy touched my face, causing me to look back at him. "It will be all right. I'm sorry it came to this, but we're together now."

"And we'll stay together," Ephesus echoed. "No matter what."

I threw my arms around Daddy and hugged him. He was right; everything would be okay. I had my family and my Bible. Maybe we couldn't go back to camp, but we could make a home somewhere else—together.

The nightmare was finally over.

9

I heard it.

I couldn't see it, but I could hear it—the sharp hiss of air, like steam escaping from a canister.

I had to find it and turn it off. There wasn't much time; already thunder was grumbling in the darkening sky, indicating the impending rain.

I ran down the street. Stanyard fell in beside me.

"It's too late!" he shouted, voice almost lost under another thunder strike. "There's enough in the air already that half the city will be destroyed."

"Then we can save the other half!" I shouted back.

He didn't respond, and his footsteps faded from beside me. Maybe he ran down another street to search there. I couldn't tell; the clouds above had grown so dark I could barely see.

But I didn't need to see. I just listened, straining to catch the unmistakable hiss over the whistling wind.

I followed the sound around a corner. And there, in a plaza at the center of town, was the container.

It was massive, blocking the road like a beached submarine. The metal side was peppered with valves, all of which were cranked fully open. The shriek of invisible gas pumping into the air made my ears ring.

I grimaced and tried to focus around the thrumming in my head. I stumbled over to the canister, hacking in the cloud of gas, and felt my hand along one of the valves. There had to be a way to shut them off!

I looked around. There—in the building across the street was a control room. I could see the dashboard of levers and knobs through the windows.

A lightning strike suddenly crashed somewhere close—too close. The flare of white light blinded me, and I nearly stumbled with the impact of the thunder. I staggered forward, blinking the colored spots out of my eyes. The storm was upon me, but if I could get inside the control room, I'd be safe.

I let adrenaline work for me as I ran over and yanked on the door handle for all I was worth.

It didn't open.

I slammed my body into the glass, panic replacing the adrenaline. "Let me in!" I wailed, even though I knew nobody was inside.

I was wrong. I heard a muffled voice from the other side of the glass. "It's too late, Miss Philadelphia."

I looked up. It was Dr. Nic's voice, but I didn't see him. Someone else was inside the control room.

"Daddy!" I shrieked.

He didn't answer, but I doubted he could hear me. He was bracing himself against the dashboard, head hanging. His eyes looked so tired and bloodshot that I was worried he was going to pass out. What had they done to him?

Never mind that. He could let me in, and we could shut off the machine. "Daddy, Daddy!" I banged on the glass.

Daddy glanced at me, but someone abruptly stepped between us. Dr. Nic stood at the door and gazed down at me, arms crossed in a stance I knew all too well. I took one step back instinctively.

"It's too late," he repeated.

I believed him. He wouldn't shut off the machine, but surely he wouldn't leave me out here in the rain! "Let me in!" I cried, yanking on the door handle for emphasis.

"So you can shut down my operation again? I don't think so." His tone wasn't triumphant, but the disconnected calmness in his voice was even more disturbing.

I stared at him. *He wouldn't. He wouldn't!*

"No, please! Let me in! Please! Daddy!" I pressed my face against the glass, struggling to get a glimpse of my father. "Daddy!"

Daddy walked up and touched Dr. Nic's arm, looking at him pleadingly. Dr. Nic shrugged him off. "She had her chance. If she had joined the project when she had the opportunity, she would be in here with you."

Joined the project? I looked to Daddy. He would never join Dr. Nic's project!

Daddy wasn't looking at me. He gazed at the floor as he turned and trudged back to the control panel.

No.

Then it started to rain. I knew not because I felt the drops—but because I *heard* them. A crackling sizzle somewhere across the street. First softly, then louder. Then a scream.

I looked over my shoulder. The street behind me was wet, not with water, but with a bubbling, steaming pool of bright orange-red acid. More drops fell from the sky like dripping blood.

And the wind was blowing towards me.

I turned and pounded my fists into the glass. "Daddy, let me in!"

He wasn't listening. He was bent over the control panel, sliding a dial.

"Daddy, how could you?" I whimpered. Betrayal flooded me, followed by hope. "Daddy, shut it off! Shut it off!" I raised my voice as loud as I could. "Shut it off!"

He looked up at me, eyes so sunken it looked like he was nearly dead. "Philadelphia, it's the only way," he said, so quietly I could barely hear him.

"Daddy!" I wailed, not sure what else to utter. "Daddy, Daddy, *Daddy*!"

I heard the sizzling acid creep up behind me like a vat of quicksand. I rammed myself into the door—my fists, my elbows, anything, as hard as I could—willing the glass to break. I prepared myself for the sharp pain of broken glass cutting my skin, and it came. Pain seared up my arms, and I screamed.

But the glass hadn't broken. I looked down to see the vile red liquid dripping off my arm, leaving a horrible burn.

More splashed against my face, my hands, my legs. I screamed again and again as the horrible sensation of scalding wetness drowned my senses.

I crumbled to the floor, my sense of touch quickly leaving me. There was nowhere to run.

No one could escape Red Rain.

"Philli, Philli!"

"Ephesus?" I gasped, unable to place the voice. "Stanyard?"

"Philli, it's me. Daddy."

It was him. His voice sounded like he was right by my head, but I couldn't see him; I couldn't see anything but darkness and splashes of red. Had he opened the door for me?

"Daddy…" I whimpered, not having the strength to speak any louder.

"Philli," he said again. This time his voice was so loud and clear I jumped. He touched my arm, and my sense of feeling came back.

And I felt no pain.

At first, I felt nothing. Then, cold stiffness came to my bones; I was lying on something hard and unforgiving. A blanket was draped over me. And Daddy was shaking my shoulder.

"Philadelphia." I looked up into his concerned face. "What's wrong?"

It took me a minute to figure out the answer to that question. I blinked, and the darkened ceiling above Daddy's head came into focus, causing me to remember where I was.

I let out a sigh and relaxed against the concrete. "Nightmares."

Daddy rubbed my shoulder. "About?" he prodded.

I glanced back up at him. He looked almost as tired as he had in the nightmare.

I cringed as the events of the dream came back to me in full color. I should tell him. He would want to know.

But I didn't want to. How could I tell him he had become a nightmare to me?

I avoided his gaze, curling back up under the blanket. "Just… everything that's been going on," I fudged.

He grunted in understanding and rubbed my shoulder consolingly. His fingers felt cold. I shivered and hoped he couldn't tell.

I was grateful when the hatch to the basement opened and Stanyard called down to us, distracting my father from further conversation.

My gratefulness vanished when I realized Stanyard was yelling in panic.

"Come on! We need to run, *now*!"

He was loud enough that he roused Ephesus and Cea from their sleep. Ephesus mumbled something generic, but Cea was upright and alert in a heartbeat. "Where's Nic?"

I think that's when we all realized Nic was no longer in the basement. And given the fact that Stanyard had ordered us not to leave the room, I think I subconsciously understood what was going on.

Stanyard confirmed my suspicions when he snapped at Cea, "Your brother decided it was a good idea to hack some government sites on the public wifi where everyone could see him. And judging by the sites he hacked, I don't think the United will have any trouble figuring out it's him."

Ephesus had fully woken by this time and joined us in collectively staring at Stanyard in disbelief. Even Cea couldn't find anything to say.

Stanyard jumped down the ladder and dropped his voice to an authoritative whisper. "We need to move immediately. Nic's hacking no doubt raised huge red flags in the United's system, so it won't take them long to investigate it and track the internet usage to here. I need you all out of here by the time they get here—if they find anything amiss, we're *all* done for."

By the time he finished, we were all standing. Ephesus and Cea were already scrambling for belongings.

"Where are we going?" Daddy asked with firm calmness.

"A rendezvous point across town. We just need to get you off the premises while the United looks around. Hopefully when they don't find you or the computer here they'll assume you were just passing through and using the area wifi. If they pin me with harboring you, I don't know what I'll do."

My heart lurched. "Where are you going?"

Stanyard looked at me. "I'm going with you. You need to use my car, and it will look suspicious if I'm here but my car's gone. The shop doesn't open until 11, so I have a few hours' window before they'll expect me to be back."

"We're ready." Ephesus stepped up with a bag slung over his shoulder, looking fully prepared. "How many will fit in your car?"

Stanyard opened his mouth, but Daddy interrupted him. "All of us." Stanyard turned to him with a frown, but Daddy returned the look with one of parental authority. "We're staying together."

The frustration burned darkly in Stanyard's eyes as he snapped, "Then some of you will be going without seat belts. Let's go." Without another word, he turned around and scrambled up the ladder. Cea followed him without hesitation.

"Philli."

I turned and brushed arms with Ephesus as he leaned close to me. He pressed something cold and small into my hands.

"Keep this on you," he said in a voice designed to prevent overhearing, even though the only other person in the room was Daddy.

I flipped the device between my fingers; it was an old flash drive. "What's this?"

"It's some of my files," he said. "If something happens, they'll definitely take my bag." He shifted the duffle protectively. "I don't want all my work in one place."

The foreboding implications of his words should have disturbed me, but adrenaline was clouding my ability to think of anything but the present. Images of spies hiding knives and guns in their shoes came to me, and I slid the drive inside my sock and wedged it down into my sneaker. I felt silly copying what I'd seen on TV, but Ephesus smiled encouragingly.

Daddy laid a hand on my shoulder. "Are you ready?"

I threw a glance around the room, startled by the question. What did I have to prepare? I hadn't brought anything with me when we broke out of the apartment complex.

I pressed my hands against my pocket to make sure my reader was still there. "I'm ready," I said with as much brave confidence as I could muster, even though my heart was starting to flutter rapidly.

He nodded and gestured for me to climb up the ladder ahead of him.

I stole a quick glance at Stanyard's bedroom—if you could call it that—as we ran through the upper basement. The stairs took us to the hallway behind the shop, which was cluttered with teetering stacks of supplies.

"You can't go into the shop," Stanyard warned in a whisper, standing in the hallway as if to block the way. "Regulations require security cameras to be placed in all businesses. I managed to block the one in the hallway with supplies." He pointed towards the exterior door. "Wait in the garage. Keep quiet and stay below the windows. I'm going to make it look like I went grocery shopping." He turned and darted off down the hallway.

Daddy took my hand and led me towards the door. We stepped into the garage just in time to hear Cea slap her brother in the face.

A brief bitter argument ensued, but Ephesus stepped between them. "Hey, save it for when you don't have to whisper."

Cea scowled like a bulldog but remained silent. Dr. Nic looked merely annoyed and not nearly concerned enough for the severity of the situation.

The door slammed seconds later, and Stanyard came out jangling keys. "Everyone in. Who's volunteering to ride in the trunk?"

I wondered if that was sarcastic, but Cea instantly responded, "Nic and I will." I was even more surprised when Nic didn't argue.

Stanyard popped the hatch on his green car. "Okay. The rest of you will have to get down on the floor. If they watch the security cameras to see when I leave, they can't see that there's anyone else with me in the vehicle."

Guess we're all going without seat belts. I glanced at Daddy in alarm. He didn't look happy about it either, but he didn't object and guided me towards the car.

Ephesus managed to fit creatively on the floor in front of the passenger's seat. I got in next and curled up on the floor behind the driver's seat. Daddy got in from the other side and laid down with his arms over me protectively. I squeezed his hand, but it didn't make me feel any more secure.

Stanyard slammed the trunk and climbed in the driver's seat. My stomach lurched as the car rocked and rumbled noisily to life. My uneasiness was not at all abated by the fact that Stanyard's car was obviously and audibly a clunker.

Stanyard paused for a split second to adjust the controls. I couldn't see him from my position, but I heard him take in a breath and let it out. "Hang on tight," he said by way of warning.

I heard the garage door groaning open. Stanyard pulled the car out slowly. I gasped and braced my hands against the seat as the car lurched down the incline of the driveway.

Stanyard braked at the street and flicked his turn signal on. He let it click irritatingly for what seemed like an unusually long time. Was the road that busy? I couldn't hear much traffic.

"Coast clear?" Ephesus ventured after a moment.

Stanyard swore for an answer.

Daddy and I both stiffened. "What?" Ephesus hissed.

"Either Nic was on the computer longer than I realized, or the United really wants him back. Three squad cars approaching." He drummed his fingers on the steering wheel before abruptly switching the signal off and turning. "I wonder what the chance of them chasing me is if I pull out slowly?" he remarked with dry amusement.

I swallowed and held my breath to keep my stomach down as we turned onto the road. For a few seconds, the ride was smooth as Stanyard casually accelerated.

And then I heard glass shattering.

I screamed and covered my head as a few pieces of glass flew. Someone else yelled, and the car swerved. I looked up to see a spiderweb spreading through the glass of the rear window.

"Well, that answers that question!" Stanyard muttered, and slammed on the gas.

I shrieked as the car revved forward, shoving me into Stanyard's seat. Daddy shook my shoulder. "Get up and buckle your seat belt, now."

I struggled to obey, but Stanyard shouted back at us. "You're less likely to get shot if you stay down there!"

"Stay down, Dad," Ephesus urged us from the front.

I curled into a ball, pressing myself flat against the floor. I felt Daddy lay down on top of me, shielding my head with his chest.

The car continued to race forward, faster and faster. I could just barely hear sirens over the groan of the engine laboring furiously.

The car suddenly wrenched around a corner. I involuntarily cried out in fear at the violent motion. *Please don't crash. We'll all lose if you crash.*

"Where are we going now?" Ephesus yelled.

"Still the rendezvous point, if we can lose them!" Stanyard returned, sounding like he was talking through gritted teeth. "Looks like I'll just be staying with you all."

My heart shriveled in grief. *What are we going to do now?* I slid my hands over my face, even though I couldn't see much of anything anyway.

The car swerved again. "Drive safely!" my dad urged, echoing my thoughts.

"Not an option!" Stanyard fired back.

"Can you try losing them on the freeway?" Ephesus suggested.

"Not enough traffic this early in the morning." Stanyard braked roughly before making what felt like an almost 180-degree turn.

"Try the—whoa!" Ephesus broke off in a yell.

"Ephesus, are you all right?" my father shouted.

"Yeah," he replied, although his voice was noticeably shaken. "They're still firing."

I heard the shots firing outside the car. I could only hope they weren't peppering the trunk with bullet holes.

"We could try that back street. Park the car behind a business and let them blaze past."

"Can't—they sent a car down the side street. Saw them."

"You have to get where they can't see you turn—this street is too wide open."

"I know that! But I can't turn here!"

They continued to bicker, voices deteriorating into chaos. I covered my ears. *Please, God, please.* I struggled to take deep breaths. It didn't help that I could feel my father's chest shaking.

"Here! Turn here!" Ephesus yelled.

Stanyard did. And then we crashed.

Everything happened all at once. The car lurched so hard I lost my sense of direction. My father's weight pressed down on me as he fell. Several people yelled. I think I screamed. Above it all I could hear the hideously distinct sound of metal crunching. Glass shattered.

And then everything became abruptly still. For an eerie moment, nothing moved, and there was no sound except for the distant wailing of sirens.

Then my father groaned and struggled to sit up. "Philli?" He shook my shoulder. "Philli, are you all right?"

I wasn't even sure how to answer the question. I slowly lifted my head and looked around. "I... think so."

I became aware of Stanyard muttering in the front. I turned to see Ephesus slumped into the passenger seat, hands pressed against his bloody face.

"Ephesus!" I shrieked.

"Son!" Daddy echoed my cry. He started to rise, then turned and pressed a hand on my shoulder. "Stay here. We're waiting for the officers to arrive. I'm not letting either of you get hurt anymore." He sat up and threw his door open.

The meaning of his words sank into me. "We're turning ourselves in? But what about Stanyard and Cea?"

"Don't move!" was the firm reply. He scrambled out of the car and opened the passenger door, bending over Ephesus.

I sat up and looked around for Stanyard. He was struggling to force the driver's door open; it was jammed against a dumpster. With several swift kicks he managed to get the door open just enough for him to squeeze through. He jumped out and yanked my door open.

"Let's go! We can escape on foot through the alleys. They can't take their cars down here, so we still have a chance of losing them."

I scrambled up and looked out. It appeared as though we had raced around the corner into an alley and hit a dumpster. I could hear the sirens still approaching us from the main road, but the alley was a clear shot. We could easily run.

But just as I grabbed the door to step out, I heard Daddy's voice behind me and halted.

No. We were not running again. Daddy said—

Before I could even finish the thought, Stanyard's urgent cry countered it. "Come on, Phil! We have to go, now!"

"Philli, come over here!" Daddy called. His voice sounded so distant and squeaky.

Stanyard held out his hand to me.

"Philadelphia!"

We could stop running. We could end this game of cat and mouse.

"Phil, if you don't come now I'll leave you behind!"

Or we could escape and perhaps never have to play this game again.

I reached out and grasped Stanyard's hand.

I was a second too late.

A shot fired somewhere in my peripheral. I had barely registered the noise before pain ripped through my leg.

I screamed and stumbled forward, falling out of the car. My head hit the ground so hard I could barely feel the sensation of the concrete scraping my face and my arms.

I saw Stanyard standing over me and was able to remember that I had to get up *now*. I tried to sit up and abruptly realized what had happened when I found my right leg was completely numb and immobile.

I had been hit by a stun shot. Now I *couldn't* run. I looked to Stanyard in a panic.

He kept his word. He turned around and ran, leaving me behind.

"Stanyard!" I cried, wheezing and nearly choking. All the wind had been knocked out of me. Stanyard disappeared around a building without looking back.

I slumped back on the ground, my clouded emotions suddenly venting themselves as tears. I heard shouts and sirens and orders from all directions, but it seemed like an inordinately long time before an officer bothered to come around the car and pick me up. Somehow that made the wound burn all the worse.

The officer scooped me up in his arms without a word. He was big and strong, and that made me feel all the more pitiful. *You're a fool. Such a fool!* I started to cry.

"Philadelphia!" My father was beside us. His hands were cuffed, but he didn't seem to mind as he reached up and stroked my forehead. "Are you all right? What were you doing?"

His tone was more condescending than concerned, like he was disappointed I had even considered making a break for it.

I sobbed harder.

"Philli, Philli." Daddy's tone changed to the one of gentle love I so craved, though I could barely hear it around the buzzing in my head. "It will be all right. I'm here." He kissed the top of my head and then found my hand.

I squeezed his hand and struggled to dam my emotions. It would be all right, I told myself. As long as we went quietly, everything would be fine. No more running. No more secrets and guns and bloodshed. And our family would be together again.

That's what was most important, I reminded myself. I needed to be with my family, no matter where that took me. This wasn't about escaping or finding freedom. This was about keeping my family together. That's what Daddy would say.

And yet, glancing back down the alley where Stanyard had fled, I couldn't help but wonder if I had my priorities wrong.

10

I was wrong.

Turning ourselves in didn't do any good. Daddy and I weren't even able to stay together. As soon as we reached the station, they split us up, because of course male and female prisoners had to be separated.

They put me in a holding cell and did just that—hold me. They didn't even bother to search me, make me sign paperwork, or give me a prison uniform. They just shoved me in, closed the door, and walked away.

They didn't allow me to send a message to my father. They never even told me how Ephesus was doing or how bad his injuries were. They just left me alone in my cell, which was even tinier and more deplorable than the one at the apartment complex, to wait until they gave me my sentence.

There wouldn't be a trial. I had forfeited that formality long ago by refusing to sign the file. Not that there was anything to stand trial on; there was no denying what I had done. I had been condemned since I broke out of the apartment building. Now it was just a matter of the officials deciding what to do with me.

I knew being sent quietly back to camp was no longer an option, but I didn't know what other options existed. I didn't want to imagine the possibilities and, in a way, I wasn't sure it mattered what they did to me. I had already lost the only thing that was important to me—the privilege to live with my family. Where I was sent now hardly made a difference.

At the moment, it looked like they wouldn't bother to send me anywhere and would just leave me to suffer in prison until they were motivated to process my paperwork; it had been three days without a word of contact from the officials.

I spent those days crying bitterly off and on. It was over. Surrendering had ended the game of cat and mouse, but it ended with the cat eating the mouse. I was a fool to think it would ever be any other way.

It was a great mercy when, on the fourth day, the United sent a guard down to talk to me.

"You have been sentenced to prison for life," he said without any other greeting. This was hardly news to me; I had been in one form of prison or another for the past five years.

"You are being transferred to the facility on Rott immediately," he continued. The name meant nothing to me, but what was one prison from another?

The guard pressed his thumb on the keypad and opened the door to my cell. I guess he meant "immediately" literally.

I stood up and followed him without a word. I didn't need to do anything to get ready. I had nothing except for the clothes on my back—and my reader, which I had managed to keep concealed in my pocket.

The guard led me through the sterile white halls to a little visiting room, where another guard met us at the door. "You have been permitted to see your father," he informed me.

I jolted out of my stupor with a sudden resurgence of hope. Maybe Daddy was coming with me. Maybe God had given us a way to be together after all.

"Ten minutes," the guard warned, and pushed the door open.

I ran through it. "Daddy!" I cried.

He was the only one in the room. He sat at the far end of a bare conference table, one hand cuffed to the metal chair. He didn't call out as I approached, but as soon as I was beside him he put his free arm around me and kissed me on the head.

"Philadelphia," he whispered.

I knelt by his chair. "I've been sentenced to Rott," I said, talking quickly to make the most of the time.

He stroked my hair. "I know. They told me."

I looked into his face. "Are you coming with me?"

He shook his head. "I haven't received my sentence yet."

The hope started to drain from my heart, making it beat faster. "Maybe they'll send you and Ephesus there too," I said, still grasping at the chance, "and then we can be together."

"I doubt it," was his quiet reply.

I doubt it? What kind of response was that? "Why wouldn't they send you to prison too?"

He just shrugged.

I struggled to maintain a calm tone of voice. "Daddy, we have to hope. God kept us together when you were sent to Mars—He can keep us together now." I grasped his free hand between both of mine. "Try asking them. Maybe they will because we're family."

"You know they won't listen, Philadelphia," he said with a sigh.

I knew it was true, but what did it hurt to try? It was our only chance. "Dad, please. Just ask them. It's our only hope—I'm not going to be coming back from Rott."

"I know," he replied.

I know? Was that all he could say? I looked up into his face, searching for more.

He pulled his hand out of my grasp and reached up to touch my cheek. He studied me for a long moment before he whispered, "I'm sorry, Philadelphia. There's nothing I can do. Nothing."

I remembered the last time he had said those words to me: When he told me that he was being sent to a base on Mars, and I was not permitted to accompany him. When he was sending me to live with complete strangers because he didn't know if he would ever be back. When we had no choice but to allow the United to split us apart.

I didn't want to believe that this was the same situation. I didn't want to admit that the only option was to say goodbye.

Daddy stroked my cheek. "It will be all right."

I didn't believe him this time. It wouldn't be all right. Not now. Not ever.

"Behave. Be polite."

No. Not this again. I won't do this again!

"Just do as they say. Go with them quietly and they'll go easier on you."

No, they wouldn't. They never had. Surrendering never worked. Surrendering got us contained in a camp, and now it had brought us here.

I wouldn't surrender again while they tore my family apart for good.

"No, Daddy, we can't do this. I won't leave you!"

"We don't have a choice."

"Daddy, please! We have to do something!" I stood up and grabbed his arm. "Just ask them! Just try for once, please!"

"Philli—"

"I'm not going quietly!" I declared, fairly shrieking. "I'm not going to just stand by and let them rip us apart again. We have to *do* something. Please, Daddy, help me!" I yanked on his arm, begging him to move, to stand, to do something, anything. "Daddy, please!"

"Hey!" One of the guards grabbed my arm and pulled me back. "That's enough. Time's up."

"No!" I screamed, struggling against him in every way I knew how.

I managed to land a good kick on his shin. With a growl he shoved me to the floor, causing me to ram my chin on the tile.

"Behave," he ordered from above.

I pushed myself to my knees, wiping a smear of blood off my lips. "No," I said, this time coldly collected. *Not this time.* I took a deep breath and rose.

"I won't go," I said calmly. I stepped in front of Daddy's chair, shielding him. "We're a family. Splitting us isn't right, and you know it."

"Girl—" the guard started to warn me, but I cut him off.

"Think about what you're doing! You're breaking apart a family and sending a woman off to prison alone. How is that right? How is that a fair punishment for what I've done?"

Both of the guards stepped towards me, as if I would find that threatening. "You have been sentenced—" one started.

"I'm not asking what your superiors told you—I'm asking if you think this is right! If you have to send us to prison, why can't you send us both to the same place? What will that hurt? How's that any different than keeping him locked up here? All I'm asking is that you put in a word—"

"Philli," Daddy interrupted, the softness of his tone causing me to stop and turn to face him.

He stared into my eyes and said, "Just go. Please. Before you get hurt."

Just go. Not "Goodbye." Not "I love you." Not even "I'm sorry."

Just go.

I, for my part, could find nothing to say.

The guards took advantage of my sudden silence and dragged me away. Daddy watched me go. I searched his eyes for the reassurance his words had lacked, but his expression wasn't teary. It wasn't even shocked. It was just tired. Tired and weary.

It wasn't until after the door had slammed and locked between us that my own emotions began to flow again. Tears blurred my vision as the guards continued to shove me down the hall. I didn't care. I didn't need to watch where I was going, so I kept my head down and allowed myself to be led along.

The guards started bickering. Something about transporting me. I only started listening when a voice I knew joined the conversation.

"That's already been arranged."

Recognition made me look up and focus on the face. Shock briefly dried my tears.

Commander Ambrose stood over me. The cold, professional expression I was used to seeing him wear had been replaced by an unreservedly delighted sneer.

My nerves snapped out of their grief when I realized things could still get worse. Much worse.

"I will be escorting her to Rott personally," he chirped. He hooked his arm with mine and swept me down the hall. Had he not been pinching my arm deliberately, one would have thought by his tones and actions that he was talking me out on a date.

The very idea made my stomach reel.

He led me out of the building to a waiting car. He opened the passenger door with a flourish. "Won't you sit up with me so we can have a chat?"

My utter disgust was making me feel defiant, so I quickly slipped into the back seat, opening the door for myself and slamming it resolutely.

I instantly regretted my decision when, not seconds later, a guard opened the opposite door and deposited a handcuffed Dr. Nic in the backseat.

Suddenly sitting shotgun with Commander Ambrose seemed like a good option.

Dr. Nic glared at Commander Ambrose so viciously that the arch of his eyebrows looked downright painful. After a moment of concentrated hatred, he seemed to realize there was someone beside him and glanced sideways. When he spotted me, his gaze focused into a look that was far worse than the one he had just given Ambrose.

I wished he come right out and say, *"You just turned this into pure torture for me."* It would have taken far less effort than contorting his face the way he was.

Unfortunately, despite my best attempts, I was probably giving him the same look.

A glance at Commander Ambrose's grin in the review mirror confirmed that he had planned it this way.

This *was* torture. Specialized torture devised just for me, simply because Commander Ambrose had a grudge and enough political weight to achieve vengeance. His personal agenda was probably the only reason I was getting sent to Rott while my family was left behind.

Grief nipped at my cheeks. I sucked in my breath and turned to face the window. I forced thoughts of my family out of my mind and instead brooded over the injustice. I raved inwardly about how this was all Commander Ambrose's fault because he hated me, elaborating on how absurd and unfair this all was. They weren't very charitable thoughts, but they kept me from succumbing to fear. I was sure my dad would agree—

No. My dad had no expectations on my behavior anymore. As far as he was concerned, I had flown the nest.

I was on my own.

11

Mercifully, Ambrose was content to savor his victory in silence as he drove us to our destination. I had assumed mutual distaste would keep Dr. Nic and me from attempting any small talk, but to my surprise, he was the first to break the silence.

"It's an island," he declared after about fifteen minutes.

"What is?" I said, venturing a glance at him. He seemed to have cooled off considerably; his livid scowl had been replaced by a frown of cold boredom as he stared out the window at the nondescript highway.

"Rott," he replied. "The prison. It's an island." He paused, then added, "I've been there," as if he had anticipated my next question.

He didn't offer any more information, and even this revelation quickly became redundant. As soon as we came in sight of a military dock filled with various United ships, I made the intelligent deduction that our prison must involve water.

Being surrounded by open sea was certainly as effective a containment method as any.

Several guards approached the car and helped Commander Ambrose escort us to a waiting ship. Ambrose led the way, brandishing his badge at all the nearby officials, although none of them were asking for it. I realized in retrospect how idiotic he looked: a pompous, over-decorated commander leading a sorry parade, as though capturing a few riffraff criminals was something to be proud of.

Aside from Ambrose's gleeful display, there was very little ceremony to our boarding. We were led up the gangplank, checked off on a ledger, and shoved over to a corner where Ambrose kept a needlessly close eye on us until the ship launched. My heart lurched with the deck when the ship detached from the dock, but I was more worried about Ambrose's constant stare than the receding shoreline.

I kept waiting for something to happen—for them to handcuff me, or put a tracking device on me, or lead us off to cells. This was a prison ship, wasn't it?

Instead, the opposite happened. As soon as the ship had chugged far enough out to sea that swimming back to land wasn't a feasible option, Commander Ambrose approached Dr. Nic. Dr. Nic's eyes flitted defensively as he watched Commander Ambrose's every move, but he didn't flinch as the bulky guard leaned over him. With an annoying beep from a handheld device, Dr. Nic's handcuffs dropped off.

Commander Ambrose stepped back and gestured at the open deck. "Enjoy your voyage," he said, still too gleeful to be considered sane. "You can go below deck in the main hold, or you can savor the view."

Without waiting to see what our choice was, he sauntered off and disappeared into an officer's cabin.

I stayed still for a long minute, still stunned with confusion. Were they not afraid that we might try to escape?

Only when I heard a cold splash on the water, followed by callous laughter and shouts of *"First!"* from the guards, did I realize that their intent was quite the opposite: If we wanted to jump overboard, we were quite welcome to.

"Tempting," Dr. Nic muttered, "but I'd rather not go out freezing. I'm going below deck out of the wind."

I'm not sure why he was telling me, especially when he didn't wait for a response before walking away. I didn't follow him.

I stayed on deck all night. I'm sure sitting out in the cold wind, being sprayed by the occasional stray wave, did not help my vain pursuit of sleep. But I didn't want to go below deck. Somehow it seemed safer to stay up top, in sight of the security lights and the night watch, than to go down below in the open hold with all the other prisoners.

Finding sleep down there would have been impossible, anyway. Might as well stay on deck, where I had found a somewhat sheltered spot between some shipping containers and a ventilation pipe.

Sleep never came, but I didn't bother looking for it. I wished I could have read my Bible, but I was worried the glow of the screen would arouse the suspicion of the guards. So I spent most of the night with my knees pulled up to my chest, my hands pressed against my reader in my pocket.

Watching the sunrise was a bittersweet affair. On one hand, I thanked God for the return of the daylight to brighten the deck and warm the air. On the other hand, the sunshine also brought the other prisoners back to the surface.

I ignored the call for first meal. I wasn't keen on giving away my position. The rations probably weren't worth the effort, anyway. I stayed curled up in my hidey-hole, hoping to go unnoticed and ignored.

When no one approached me for the better part of the morning, I decided to risk taking out my reader. What good was having it if I was never able to read it? I kept the screen light down and my knees pulled up, hopefully shielding the device from any nosy passerby.

I opened the bookmark to the Bible passage I had been studying last. At first I spent more time fugitively glancing around than reading, but the lull of the text soon pulled me in.

Settling back, I glazed through the chapters, idly swiping my finger across the screen to turn the pages. I wasn't studying the passages; the deeper meaning was lost on me as I devoured the book like one might scarf down a novel for pleasure. I wasn't looking for prophetic instruction this time; I just wanted the comfort of the familiar text. It was like having a friend sitting next to me in companionable silence; just looking at the words on the screen reminded me that the book—and its Author—were still near.

I became so absorbed in the rhythm that I didn't notice someone approaching until they stopped in front of me and blocked the sunlight. Startled, I jerked my head up and nearly collided with the chin of Commander Ambrose.

For a split second I was frozen in fear, partially because of the close proximity of his face to mine. But the hot foulness of his breath soon made me squirm and struggle to pull away. I tried to slide my reader into my pocket, but that second lost in fear was a second too long. Ambrose already had his hand around my wrist.

"What's this? Smuggling electronics?" he jeered with an annoying perk to his voice. He had clearly gotten plenty of sleep.

"It's mine!" I cried fruitlessly as he easily yanked the device from my grasp.

He straightened and squinted at the screen. His face lit up with that delighted sneer I had seen one too many times in the past twenty-four hours. "Oh," he crooned, "contraband."

I snarled, more out of anger than fear. "Give it back! Please," I added, briefly wondering if pleading would work on him.

He started walking away. "You know, this book is illegal to own."

I scrambled up and trotted after him, trying not to panic. "Not for unassimilated," I reminded him, hoping to hit on whatever fragment of mercy had caused him to allow us to keep our Bibles at camp. But somehow I knew that fragment of mercy didn't exist anymore, if it ever had.

He stopped by the deck railing and looked down at me. "You're not unassimilated anymore," he spat. "You're worse than that. The unassimilated are still part of the system. You've been thrown out with the trash."

I couldn't come up with a reply, partially because I knew he was right.

"That means you have no rights," Ambrose continued with unmasked glee, "and certainly no rights to own something like this." He dangled the reader above my head and wiggled it tauntingly.

I gazed at it helplessly, all the resistance gone from my system. "Please," I whispered, "just let me keep it."

He closed his large fist around the device. "And what will you do in exchange?"

I shifted my gaze to his face. Is that what this was all about? Had he truly dropped so low?

But what could I do about it? I might as well play his petty games if it meant I could keep my Bible.

"Anything," I said with total honesty.

He grinned wildly. "Tempting," he said, "but I can't think of anything I want from you." And in one swift motion, he turned and hurled my reader into the sea.

I think I screamed an objection. I could never remember. My mind wasn't on whatever pitiful exclamations may have left my mouth as I lunged forward, propelled by the desperate hope that I could catch it.

I slammed into the deck railing with my stomach and had to grab the bar with both hands to keep from falling overboard. All the wind knocked out of me, I couldn't even cry as I watched my reader hit the water with a fatal splash and sink out of sight.

I stared at the waves for several moments, vainly hoping to see it bob back to the surface. But I knew it wouldn't float. As hard as it was to process, I knew my reader was gone—and with it my only hope of ever owning a Bible again.

Ambrose approached me from behind, talking. I had no idea what he said because my mind was suddenly overcome with a ravenous thought. In one instinctive motion, I turned and punched him in the gut.

He grunted and jerked back, glaring at me with unmasked shock. I was just as surprised as he was. My hand tingled from the impact and my mind from the realization of what I had done. Then, for a very brief moment, it felt good.

That moment ended when Ambrose punched me back.

I stumbled backwards but managed to retain my balance. His next strike seemed perfectly timed to send me to the ground.

No sooner had I hit the deck then he kicked me. Twice. Three times. My head was spinning so violently I couldn't do anything but squeeze out a whimpered cry, the breath again knocked from my chest.

Ambrose paused for a moment to leer over me and issue threats. I couldn't remember his exact words, but I got the gist. *That's what happens when you sass me, girl.*

I coughed, struggling to get my breath back. Reprimands swirled around in my head, as if spoken by my father's voice. *Stop fighting. You'll only get hurt.*

Tears shot to my eyes and quickly dropped to the deck.

"Hey!"

Both Ambrose and I looked up to see Nic leaning on the deck railing nearby. He stroked his mustache casually. "I'm curious, Ambrose," he said cheerfully. "Did the United train you to hit women, or are you just that vile on your own?"

Both Ambrose and I stared at him. Was he defending me, or just enjoying the spectacle? I struggled to sit up.

Dr. Nic pushed himself off the railing and sauntered towards Ambrose. "I'll admit to being a little impressed, though. I mean, you had the guts to hit a woman in front of all these men," he gave a broad gesture at the prisoners and guards loitering around the deck, "whose protective instincts might flare up at any moment. Even I don't have the courage to do that."

Commander Ambrose gave a short laugh. It was short because Nic punched him in the stomach and cut him off.

Ambrose sputtered indignantly, but his return strike was almost immediate. But Nic's lean and swift form seemed to have an advantage over Ambrose's hefty one, and in the ensuing scuffle he managed to deal at least twice as many hits as he took.

I watched in speechless wonder. I had no idea Dr. Nic could fight like that. I was even more surprised that he would employ his skills in my defense.

I doubted either of them were getting hurt that much, but when blood spurted from Ambrose's lip, he decided he'd had enough. He roared and lunged forward, slamming all his body weight into Dr. Nic like a charging bull. Nic lost his balance and fell backwards on the deck with a grunt.

Ambrose shook himself and stomped towards Nic as he struggled to rise. Suddenly I worried that the fight was about to get ugly—if not lethal.

"Stop!" I cried before I could catch myself, but a shrill whistle blast outshouted me.

I turned to see a captain and several guards jog towards us. "Ambrose!" the captain barked. "What is the meaning of this?"

Ambrose stopped and turned to him. He seemed to struggle for a reply, long enough that Nic spoke first. "Oh, just having a friendly duel in defense of a lady," he chirped, sitting up and brushing himself off. "All in good fun."

The captain abruptly seemed to realize I was there, kneeling on the floor with my arm around my stomach. I could tell by the way his eyes widened and then darkened that he understood the situation.

"They were causing a ruckus, sir," Ambrose offered, voice noticeably shaky.

"I've no doubt about that," the captain quipped. "But that's what tasers are for. You know the regulations."

Before Ambrose could sputter out a defense, the captain added, "Or were they too much for you and your only option was to defend yourself with your fists?"

The look on Commander Ambrose's face was priceless. It took all my willpower not to smile.

Dr. Nic seemed to have no such reservations as he stood up, grinning delightedly as if he'd planned it this way all along.

The captain straightened, his voice returning to its normal bark. "Quarters, Ambrose."

"But—" he protested, looking and sounding like a child being sent to the corner.

"Did you not tell me yourself that your job is not to guard the prisoners?" the captain cut him off calmly. "So since you cannot do your job until we reach Rott, it would do me a great favor if you would stay below deck and stop interfering with my guards' work."

It was phrased as a polite suggestion, but the captain's tone and expression indicated it was anything but. Offering up no argument except a smoldering stare, Commander Ambrose turned and marched across the deck.

The captain turned back to us. "Now, what do you have to say for yourselves?"

"She started it," Nic said with a shrug.

I shot a pained glare in his direction. Now was not a good time for jokes. My glare turned into an honest grimace as I struggled to rise. I gasped and braced myself against the railing.

The captain grunted. "It seems I'll need to separate you from the other prisoners, girl. Someone is going to get hurt—most likely you, it would seem."

I looked up at him worriedly. Did he honestly think I had done something to provoke Ambrose? Was he going to punish me now?

The captain glanced at the guards behind him. "Lock her in one of the unused quarters and prohibit anyone from visiting her without my permission. That should prevent further... incidents."

"Yes, sir." One of the guards came over to assist me to my feet. "You, come with me."

I didn't dare resist as he took my arm and led me across the deck. It wasn't until we reached the door to the stairwell that I realized what the captain had done for me.

I glanced over my shoulder, but the captain had already walked away. Dr. Nic was still there, leaning against the deck railing with his arms crossed, watching me.

Had he planned it this way? Had he done this—for me?

I recalled the images of him punching Commander Ambrose in the face. I didn't have the courage to shout with all the guards listening, so simply mouthed the words *"Thank you."*

He answered me with a nod.

12

Rott was, in fact, an island, and that was really all that could be said about it.

It was a formless floating mass of land that had been razed of all vegetation. There was barely even any sand on the shore. Mismatched concrete and stone buildings crowded for space as though they were afraid they were going to fall off the edge into the ocean. There was no fence or barbed wire; again, it seemed like swimming with the fish was always a viable option.

The only thing that distinguished it as a prison was the four guard towers stationed at each perpendicular of the island. We passed under the shadow of one as we were herded off the boat and into the yard. I glanced up at the glass-walled balcony three stories above me and caught a glimpse of a lone guard idling at the controls. He was not that much older than me, with dirty blond hair he hadn't bothered to comb. He was watching the offloading prisoners with, of all expressions, a raised eyebrow.

"That's Tower."

"I can see it's a tower," I returned without looking. I knew it was Dr. Nic beside me.

"No, that's his name. The guard."

"Really?"

He shrugged.

"Is he a friend?"

Nic paused and looked up. The two men stared at each other for a good ten seconds, but if any emotion was exchanged, I missed it.

Nic looked away and continued walking. "I don't think friends will help us much in here."

I decided to resume ignoring him.

The captain shuttled us into the barracks, which was the first building on the right. I was relieved to find that all of the buildings and their subsequent halls were clearly labeled. My new quarters were marked Cell #3.8—third floor, eighth cell from the elevator. None of the prisoners had any security clearance; all doors had to be unlocked by a guard.

At least I wouldn't be getting lost in prison.

My cell wasn't that much different than the one back on the mainland. If it weren't for the irritated sound of the restless sea echoing through the drafty building, I could have imagined I was back on the shore.

As a mercy to us both, Nic was contained on another floor. However, if I was hoping my confinement would lead to some alone time, I was sorely mistaken.

Not ten minutes after I got settled in, Commander Ambrose sauntered up to my floor, again dragging Dr. Nic behind him. I assumed Nic was as frustrated as I was, but he didn't bother to belie his irritation. He just looked grossly overtired.

"I'm here to assign you to your new jobs," Commander Ambrose crooned. He seemed to have recovered from his scolding on the ship and was back to exuberantly enjoying his vacation.

Working for Commander Ambrose sounded like cruel and unusual punishment, but perhaps doing menial work was better than scratching off the days on the wall in my cell. In either case,

I decided to follow Nic's example and not betray my ragged emotions as I followed the commander down the hall.

He led us to the building at the center of the island. Even though it was the plainest and ugliest building—if that were possible—it appeared to be the most important. Ambrose had to flag us through multiple layers of security—armed guards at the door, metal detectors, even a secretary—before we descended on a dimly-lit elevator to the heart of the building.

"I'm one of the few people who has full access to this building," he reminded us at least twice. "They won't let you in without me—so don't be late for your shifts."

He resumed that self-important grin he had been practicing so much lately. I thought about asking him what would happen if I were late, but I decided not to push it on my first day at work.

The elevator stopped three floors down. As if relishing the reveal, the doors groaned open slowly, allowing our eyes to adjust to the sudden brilliance of a million fluorescent lights. They dangled from the ceiling like tired stars, illuminating an absolutely monstrous factory.

The thunder of noise hit me almost as hard as the smell of grease and sulfur. The elevator dumped out onto a railed ledge overlooking it all. Without thinking, I walked up to the edge and leaned over, taking everything in at once. Below me, dozens of machines worked overtime to the tune of hissing steam and clanking gears. Across the room, two massive holding tanks like barn silos were bolted to the wall. From their sides spawned a writhing network of pipes and gauges that crawled across the ceiling, accessible only by the swaying network of catwalks and service ladders that dangled by rusty chains.

My head spun just looking at it. It wasn't until Commander Ambrose spoke that I realized I had closed my eyes.

"You'll be working over there." He pointed across a narrow walkway that jutted out over the factory. It led to an alcove in front of the holding tanks, where the mess of gauges and dials could be accessed. From this distance, the whole platform seemed to sway, but that might have been my stomach reeling in protest.

"But I can't—" I squeaked, afraid I might vomit if I raised my voice.

"Not you," Commander Ambrose snorted. "That job's for him. I don't trust you with the equipment."

I was so relieved that I didn't even notice his heavy-handed insult.

Dr. Nic didn't seem bothered by his assignment, but he did have the gumption to ask: "What is this factory making?"

Commander Ambrose didn't respond right away, a sign that should have concerned me had I not been more focused on trying to swallow back nausea. As it was, his answer caught me off guard and nearly made me hurl from the impact.

"I'm surprised you don't recognize it," he sneered, as if the ugly tangle of machines gave any indication of their purpose. "We're making Red Rain."

13

Before replying, I spent a good five minutes genuinely contemplating the feasibility of building a boat and attempting to row towards the mainland, whatever direction that was in. I would rather attempt an improbable escape than help produce the superweapon I had worked so hard to destroy.

"Wow," Dr. Nic whispered. To his credit, he sounded—perhaps for the first time in his life—regretful. "I guess the old man really did have it."

I wanted to punch him, but strangely, I wasn't sure he deserved it. Yes, Red Rain had been his idea. But this time, he wasn't responsible for forcing my father to work on the project. The United had played their hand, and my father had folded.

My father had completed Red Rain, and there was no one else that could be blamed for that.

But as much as I wanted to cry or scream or *kill something*, my first concern was getting out of this factory. The United may have the formula for Red Rain, but they couldn't make me produce it. If they wanted to churn out a whole factory of that vile stuff, they could do it themselves.

I may be a prisoner. They may have taken everything from me. But I still had my dignity, and they would have to kill me before I worked on Red Rain.

Commander Ambrose graciously listened to my tirade for several minutes. It wasn't until halfway through that I realized was even using real words, not just seething and screaming internally like I thought I was.

"And your options are...?" he asked when he got bored enough to interrupt.

That was an excellent question, and I would have loved to know what my options were. What was he going to do? Confine me to my cell? Threaten me? Was I worth the trouble?

I glanced around the factory. Out of the corner of my eye, I spotted a control room off to the left and up a short flight of stairs. The room was dark except for a wide dashboard glittering with a dozen displays. All around the factory there were computer terminals, gauges, dials, and control switches—more than enough ways for a rebellious girl like me to tamper with the operation.

I took a deep breath. If they wanted me to slave 9-5 in this factory pushing paperwork or mopping floors, so be it. That was plenty of time for me to become familiar with the controls—and figure out a way to stall production.

Not wanting to arouse Ambrose's suspicion by resigning too early, I fired another question at him. "Why me?"

He raised his eyebrow.

"If you wanted to rub your victory in *his* face," I gestured at Dr. Nic, "I get it. But why me? Why didn't you drag Cea and Ephesus and my father here so you could gloat over all of us?"

He hesitated, as if he never expected he'd have to answer for his personal vendettas. Perhaps there truly was no reason he'd picked me other than pure hatred.

As if realizing I couldn't be fooled, he settled for a cold smile and a haughty, "There were... regulations preventing getting your father and brother here."

I crossed my arms and remained silent.

Claiming the victory, he turned away and started walking towards the control room. "Come along, I'll show you what your job is."

Leaving Dr. Nic languishing by the railing, I followed the commander up the steps. With a swipe of his card, he ushered me into the cramped room and flicked on the light.

The room thrummed with the grinding of motherboards and hard drives. It was so crowded with file cabinets and server racks that there was barely room enough for both of us to maneuver around the desk chair. Most of the equipment was brand new, glittering in shiny black, except for a surprisingly ancient laser printer in scratched cream. It was lazily spitting out paper with a content hum, like an old granny clicking away at her knitting.

"Your job is to file all the reports that print out." He gestured at the stack of paper rapidly piling up on the printer's tray.

I picked up the stack and rifled through it, wondering if any of the information would be useful. Almost immediately, the printer dispensed another five sheets in rapid succession.

"How often does it print reports?" I asked.

"Every fifteen minutes for general production, plus reports of any abnormality."

I glanced at him suspiciously. Why would the United want to keep such detailed reports in hard copy? They no doubt had access to all of this information digitally. It's not like they were going to ask Ambrose to mail his paperwork to them in a manila envelope.

An ear-piercing beep interrupted our staring contest. "Oh," he piped, "you'll also have to reload the paper."

I sighed and pulled open the paper drawer on the printer. As stupid as it was—I was beginning to suspect Ambrose was wasting paper for the sole purpose of having me do menial work in his presence—I wasn't going to complain when my "job" gave me full access to the control room *and* all of their classified reports.

I half-listened while Commander Ambrose explained the organization of the file cabinets to me. I impatiently waited for him to stop talking so I could start exploring the office and reading the reports.

I didn't have any time to waste. We had to stop production before any product was shipped back to the mainland.

Why my internal dialog thought there was a "we," I'll never know. When I approached Dr. Nic at dinner, he made it very clear that he intended to be utterly useless.

"It's too late," he muttered as he aggressively stirred his colorless food.

"No, it's not. They can't have had the factory operational for more than a few days," I reasoned, doing the math in my head. "There's no way they've already shipped a boatload back to the mainland."

"Not that," he whined, as if frustrated by my stupidity. "I mean it's too late—just, how do you propose destroying something that eats metal?"

"Why are you eating metal for lunch? The rations aren't *that* bad, except on pizza day."

I jumped, although more so because the stranger's voice was extremely loud than because I was startled. I looked up to see a curious pair of men grinning at me. They looked incredibly alike, as though they were related, but there were just enough differences between them that it made me go cross-eyed. They were both short, but one was a fraction of an inch taller. They both had white hair, but one had more gray than the other. I could have also sworn their eyes were slightly different shades of grey, but at that point I realized I was staring.

Neither of them seemed to mind, because they were both doing the same thing right back at me. "Oh, you brought a lady friend back with you! How nice!" the slightly taller one chirped.

"Dowe, she's too young for him. Don't be disgusting." The other jabbed him in the ribs.

"You're right. She could definitely do better, John."

They both paused and rubbed their chins with one hand, as if assessing potential suitors in their mind. I decided I'd better put a quick stop to their train of thought before I got set up on a blind date with a prisoner, so I spoke up, "You're John... and Dowe?" I tried not to grimace at the irony of the names.

They nodded eagerly.

"And you thought 'Tower' was a weird name," Dr. Nic muttered.

"So how you doing, Q? I didn't expect you back so soon." John and Dowe sat at the table next to us.

Nic looked up and stared them straight in the eyes. "But you did expect me back."

They shrugged and started eating.

"'Q'?" I ventured.

Nic rolled his eyes. "I wasn't going to keep going by Prisoner 120518."

"Are you... friends?" I glanced around the table at my unlikely group of prison mates.

Dr. Nic looked genuinely bored. "What did I tell you about friends?"

Dowe slapped his hands on the table so violently that our canteens sloshed. "Whatever he told you was wrong! We are definitely your friends, so don't listen to this stick-in-the-mud."

"Yeah!" John agreed. "We're way more fun than he is, anyway."

That last statement definitely wasn't a lie, so I decided to let it slide for the time being.

I looked back at Dr. Nic. "Should I tell... them?"

"Pretty sure we're not the only people on the island who know what that factory is making," he replied dryly. Then without offering further comment, he picked up his dishes, stood up, and walked away.

He didn't look at me as he passed, but I could read the expression on his face. I could tell by the look in his eyes that he truly *didn't* care what I did. He had given up, surrendered himself and his precious pet project to the hands of the United. He looked as tired as my father used to.

The thought made my heart sick in more ways than one, so I shoved it aside. Never mind Nic. If he was content to slave in a factory of his own design, let him. But I wouldn't. I wouldn't let the United have Red Rain if there was anything I could do to stop it.

But Dr. Nic had a point. How *could* you destroy something that ate metal?

John and Dowe didn't have any helpful advice to offer, even after I explained the situation to them as best I could. "Does it burn? We could burn it."

"It's a gas. You can't burn gases."

"Yes you can! Like those vintage gas stoves!"

"Not that kind of gas!"

I excused myself as soon as I politely could and locked myself in my cell. I spent the night curled up on the cot, trying to think of ways to destroy Red Rain. I didn't know how to create it, but perhaps I could think of a way to destroy it. After all, I had destroyed Dr. Nic's operations once before.

Of course, I hadn't exactly destroyed anything important then—if I had, we wouldn't be in this mess. And besides, I didn't have any tables of random chemicals I could turn over to create a makeshift bomb.

I growled and rubbed my forehead. There had to be a way! I had full access to the factory, albeit during working hours. There had to be *something* I could do to stop it.

I wished Ephesus were here. He would know how to destroy something he helped create.

A sudden wave of homesickness washed over me at the thought of my brother. What had they done to him? Had he even heard where I'd been sent?

Taking a deep breath to dam the rising tears, I closed my eyes and leaned back against the cold wall, trying to keep my thoughts on the task at hand. If Ephesus were in my place, what would he try first?

He'd hack the computer, of course. The thought made me smile at the same time it made my heart sink in despair. I could probably tamper with the computer if Ambrose left me in the control room unsupervised, but it wouldn't do me any good. Almost everything was probably password-protected, and I wouldn't know what to look for even if it wasn't. I only knew how to manage simple devices like readers and flash drives.

Flash drives! With a rush of recognition that made me sit up faster than was healthy, I remembered the flash drive Ephesus had passed to me before we got caught. It was still tucked down the side of my shoe, safe and sound—because I hadn't exactly had a reason to take my shoes off and put my feet up the past few days.

I fished it out of my sweaty sock and held it up to the bleary light. It was definitely Ephesus's drive; the initials "E.S." written in permanent marker were still faintly visible. It was a dated unlocked model he had used in school before the United had started confiscating unapproved electronics. Somehow he had managed to smuggle it into camp and had used it to store files off the cloud. He and Cea had been using it for their recent projects. I wondered what was stored on there now.

Perhaps it was time to find out.

14

"Wowee, an unlocked drive! We could really use one of those!" John crowed when I showed it to him and Dowe the next morning.

"Yeah," Dowe said, fingering it admiringly. "We need a place to store our covert files. Can we borrow it?"

"We'll be careful with it!"

"We're always careful with other people's stuff!"

"Actually, I need to figure out what's on it. My brother passed it to me before we were transported," I replied.

"Ooh, a secret message from the mainland!"

"We have just the translation device. That old laptop should work. The screen's almost history, though."

"That's because you dropped it down shaft 9. You should have taken the elevator."

"It was an undercover operation! I couldn't take the elevator! Someone might have *seen* me!"

I hated to interrupt them, but I only had a few minutes before Commander Ambrose would expect me to be down in the factory for work. "Can I borrow this laptop for a minute?"

They were right; the laptop was about ready to give up the ghost. But the USB port was still intact, and I could see enough of the screen to read the file list that popped up. I scanned the titles; regretfully, most of them meant nothing to me.

A file from the bottom of the list did catch my eye, though—it was named "Sans Nic (fixed)." I thought that was a funny name, so I clicked on it. The file extension was unusual, too.

A big warning box engulfed the screen. I read the text aloud in wonder: "'This file may contain viruses or other programs that may be harmful to your computer. Are you sure you want to run?'"

"Whoa Nellie, don't open that!" John or Dowe yelped from behind me.

"Yeah, don't destroy this laptop! It's the last one we have left!"

"We do have a couple tablets, though. And half a desktop."

"This is still the last *laptop*."

"True."

I ignored them as I pondered the warning. Why would the computer call the file out as a virus? I canceled the action and clicked on a different file out of curiosity. It opened without complaint. I looked back at the corrupted file, pondering the name. *Sans Nic... without Nic... a virus without Nic...*

I stopped. That was it. A virus without Nic. A virus that *removed* Nic.

We switched it up, though. We set it so that the virus would only delete data that contained the letters 'Nic,' with a capital.

This was the data virus my brother had coded for Nic back on Mars. He'd sabotaged it so that it would only delete data that contained Nic's name.

But now, judging by the file name, it had been fixed. That must have been one of the projects my brother and Cea had been working on back at camp. Now the virus would do what it was originally intended to do—completely wipe all data from all systems it infected.

Suddenly, I knew how we'd destroy Red Rain.

15

Dr. Nic and I didn't speak when we both showed up for work, which was just as well. From my perch in the control room, I watched him unenthusiastically monitor the gauges on the machines and briefly wondered if it would be better to leave him out of my plan. But as much as I questioned his dedication, I knew that he understood Red Rain better than I did, and it would probably be wise to get an expert opinion before I attempted to sabotage a factory full of lethal chemicals.

As we exited the elevator at the end of our shift, I cowered in the back corner so Ambrose would get off first. Letting him get a few paces ahead, I whispered to Dr. Nic, "Meet me at Tower's place after dinner."

Not waiting for his response, I skipped ahead of him and ran to mess hall to avoid Ambrose's suspicion.

After hastily scarfing down my food, I went above ground and asked Tower if he would keep watch while we met behind his building. I hadn't bothered to ask for his cooperation beforehand, partially because I had come up with the plan on the spot, and partially because now was as good a time as any to figure out whether or not Tower was an ally. As I had hoped, Tower agreed. He didn't ask what we were going to be talking about, so I didn't volunteer the information.

I promptly sat down in the shadows behind the building and waited. There was no reason to go anywhere else. Besides, I needed time to think—and pray. I needed to plan what to say if Dr. Nic showed up or, more importantly, what to do if he didn't show up, which was more likely.

I was extremely encouraged—and a little bit flattered—when he actually came.

I didn't wait for him to ask what I wanted. I stood up and declared in a low tone, "We need to destroy Red Rain."

He raised one eyebrow in a bored gesture of disbelief but said nothing. I took the opportunity to keep talking. "I have to try. I won't just stand by and watch while they destroy the world. I can't…"

I stopped. No. This wasn't about me, my emotions, or my opinions. This was about doing what was right. And if we were going to pull it off, Dr. Nic and I needed to be in it together.

"*We* can't let them do that," I rephrased, emphasizing the inclusive word.

He didn't take the bait. "Why don't you just destroy it yourself? You've done it once before," he cut dryly.

I struggled not to get frustrated and instead returned his sarcasm in kind. "There aren't any tables of chemicals I can turn over," I said with equal sass. "And I need your help."

"Why?" he demanded. His tone was still condescending, but I sensed a little bit of curiosity in his expression.

"Because I'm no good with computers," I said with total honesty, hoping that would be enough to pique his interest.

"You seem to do just fine hacking security systems."

"Only because I stole a device *you* invented."

"I'm impressed that you'll admit to stealing." He was still using the same dry tone, but he straightened and watched me as I talked.

"We need to hack the computer in Ambrose's control room." I figured I had enough of his interest to cut to the point. "From there we can wipe their data and shut down the operation."

"Even if... even *after* I hack into the computer, it will be incredibly difficult to erase the data such that it's irretrievable. It is almost impossible to permanently delete information from a computer."

I was immensely pleased to hear him discussing the situation with rationality. "I know. But this will do it for you." I drew my brother's flash drive from my pocket and held it up.

He gazed at it. "What good will that do? That has all the Red Rain files on it too, you know."

"What?" I gasped.

"I transferred the complete research files from the lab before we escaped," he said with utter calmness. "I'm sure the United added a bit after we left, but I could easily figure it out from your father's notes."

Horror swept over me as I realized I had been guarding the complete formula for Red Rain in my shoe, but Nic continued talking. "But how is that going to help us destroy their operation?"

I clenched the drive, resisting the urge to run to the shore and throw it into the sea. "It also contains my brother's virus."

After a few seconds of dull staring, recognition flashed across Dr. Nic's eyes. "The data virus."

"Yes," I said, watching his face to see his reaction. "He and Cea fixed it."

Dr. Nic's expression brightened in surprise, but he quickly covered it with a scowl. "So the little twerp *did* know how to code it properly."

I gracefully ignored the slander on my brother's name and kept talking. "Yes, and if you upload it to the computer in the control room, it will completely wipe their systems."

I waited for him to commit or argue. When he did neither, I added, "Hopefully it's a closed system so nothing else will be affected."

Thoughtfulness cloaked Dr. Nic's voice again. "Yes, no doubt it's a very secured private system, but if we're lucky the gates won't be too hard to crack. They must have some way they're transmitting progress reports back to the mainland. If we can find out how, hopefully we can use that access to open a two-way door."

He looked up at me and explained, "Wiping the control system in the factory won't be enough. The United will have copies of the research on their mainland computers. Even if we destroy the factory, they can rebuild it. If we want to stop them from producing Red Rain, we need to wipe all their systems."

Panic rose in my throat as his voice gained velocity. "If we're going to do this, we have to do it right. We need to hack through the computer and upload the virus to the internet, wiping everything. We have to erase Red Rain from their systems for good!"

Tower shushed him from above. Dr. Nic ducked his head and lowered his voice, but his tone retained its vehemence. "We have to use the virus as it was originally intended."

"But that will erase everything!" I blurted the obvious, unable to contain it. "The Bibles—"

"Then why did your brother create the virus?" Dr. Nic challenged. "He didn't have to rewrite it. Why would he code it and keep it on hand, if it wasn't for a situation like this? We have to use it."

He reached for the drive. I retracted my hand.

Dr. Nic grunted and clenched his fist like he might force the drive from me. He raised his arm, then stopped. He lifted his head and gazed at me.

And he waited.

I pressed the drive against my heart. It was my choice. My choice whether or not to use the virus. My choice whether or not to trust Nic.

After thinking a quick prayer, I held the drive out.

His hand closed around it, and our eyes met. Respect briefly flashed across his face. I nodded and lowered my arm, closing the deal.

"This still won't be enough," he said lowly. "We have to destroy the product they've already made."

"Why?"

"For one, there's enough in there already to desecrate a small country. I did the calculations during my shift today. And two, there's a risk they can reconstruct the formula from a completed sample. We have to destroy their reserves so there's no trace left."

I agreed, but that didn't make the feat any less daunting. "How are we supposed to destroy something that can eat metal?" I threw his own words back at him.

He stopped and stared profoundly at the wall above my head. I let his brain work in silence for several moments.

My patience was rewarded when he mumbled, "We let it burn."

"What?"

Realization brightened his eyes as he explained, "We drain the vats. If we can release the acid and get it to condense, Red Rain will burn through the floor and destroy itself."

Let Red Rain destroy itself. We both reveled in the brilliant irony of that for a moment before Dr. Nic continued. "We'll need to get Ambrose out of the factory during working hours when all the systems are open and online."

"How?" I said, hoping his genius mind would work wonders again.

"How about a distraction?" a cheerful voice joined the conversation.

I gave a small shriek as John and Dowe materialized out of the shadows. "Tower!" Dr. Nic hissed up at the guard's window.

"I didn't think they were a problem," came the reply.

The pair sauntered over to us. "How about a distraction?" John repeated.

"A big one," Dowe clarified.

"We could do a demonstration!"

"Those are always fun!"

"We could make it like a talent show, and Philli here can help us. I bet she can put on a real good distraction!"

Dowe slapped his partner. "Don't be a fool! We don't want a woman getting tangled up in a demonstration. This could get messy."

"We need it to be messy," Dr. Nic inserted, stepping up. He glanced between the men and nodded encouragingly. "Really messy. 'All guards on deck' messy."

The matching grins on John's and Dowe's faces indicated that they were catching on. "Oh, I think we and a couple dozen of our prison buddies can handle that," John sneered.

"Let's ask Art," Dowe suggested.

"And Marty. And that guy who calls himself 24... What's his real name again?"

"I think it's Cloud."

"How's that a real name? You sure the guy ain't duping us with a double-double alias?"

The pair continued chattering. I turned back to Dr. Nic. "Commander Ambrose always locks the control room door when he leaves," I offered, my mind suddenly racing through all the possible hitches to our plan. "What if he takes the time to lock it?"

"If that happens, you can figure out a way to circumvent the lock." It wasn't a question.

I didn't argue. "When should we do it?"

"Tomorrow," Tower suddenly inserted into the conversation. I looked up to see him leaning out his window. "A ship is coming at noon to transport the first batch of Red Rain. If you want to keep the reserves out of the hands of the United, you need to destroy it before that ship comes."

I glanced at Dr. Nic. The despondent look on his face set all my worries whirling into a tornado in my stomach. "Tomorrow is my floor's 'day off.' We're all forcibly confined to our quarters. For lack of a better phrase, I'll be locked in my room." It was a fitting expression; he looked about as grumpy and pathetic as a disobedient child in timeout.

I grappled for encouraging words, but no immediate solution came to mind. Even with my knack for breaking through locked doors, I knew that getting onto his floor would be nearly impossible. Someone with access would have to let Nic out of his room.

I glanced up at Tower's window. He was still leaning there, gazing at me. I wondered if he too weighing in his mind whether or not he was truly on our side.

After a moment, he slid back inside his tower, but his voice came floating down to us. "I'll make it happen." With that, he slammed his window shut, cutting off my opportunity to thank him.

I turned back to Dr. Nic. He nodded. "We have less than 18 hours," he said, taking a deep breath. "Better get back to our cells before we arouse suspicion for being up here."

"Good point," John agreed with a yawn. "See you tomorrow."

"Don't let the bed bugs bite!" Dowe added by way of goodbye.

The two sauntered off without being bidden. Not in a rush to get back to my cell, I took a deep breath of the cold night air and savored the silence as an opportunity to pray.

I watched as Dr. Nic walked on ahead of me. After a moment, I realized I wasn't just praying about tomorrow.

16

I went to work as normal in the morning. At least, I tried to pretend it was business as usual. I had only been at this job two days; what did "acting casual" even look like? What kind of behavior did Commander Ambrose expect from me? Despondency? Bitterness? Fear?

Fear was easy to fake. I flinched at the commander's every move, always worried I had made a wrong step and aroused his suspicion. He did seem to notice that I was acting jumpy, but if anything, he appeared to be amused by it. For once, I wasn't bothered by his condescending pleasure. As long as he was smiling cruelly at me like he always did, I could assume I was safe from suspicion.

Thankfully, John and Dowe were punctual—and successful—and at precisely 10:15 Commander Ambrose's communicator beeped shrilly.

"What?" he answered in a dry tone with obviously no regard for the person on the other end.

"Ambrose, we need you topside immediately. The prisoners started a riot and it's getting... sticky." The guard's awkward tone of voice made me wonder if he was using that word literally. I wouldn't have put it past John and Dowe.

"That's not my job," was Ambrose's completely uninterested reply.

"The captain's called all guards on deck."

"I'm not a guard. I'm here to oversee production, not herd prisoners. Take care of your own charges."

I gave up pretending to ignore the discussion and watched, inadvertently crumpling the papers I held in my hands. I hadn't bargained on Commander Ambrose's self-authority. What if he refused to obey orders?

Heated talking came through in the background of the line. With a small cough, the guard responded, "The captain says it's topside or mainland."

I tried not to grin. I really did like this captain.

Commander Ambrose surrendered with an exasperated sigh. Clicking off his communicator, he shoved his chair back and stood up. "Get out," he commanded with a flick of his finger at me.

My panic resurged. I had been so focused on not tripping up that I'd neglected to think of a plan to get back into the office should Ambrose lock it. "But sir," I protested, "I have to finish filing these papers!" I held them out to him for emphasis, then realized I'd crumpled several. I hastily smoothed the stack.

He growled. "Fine. Don't touch the computer, or I will know about it when I look at the task log. I'll be right back." He stormed out. I watched him disappear into the elevator and finally released my pent-up breath in a prayer of thanks.

I could only hope that Commander Ambrose *wouldn't* be right back.

Now all I had to do was wait for Dr. Nic to arrive.

Waiting turned out to be harder than pretending to act casual. At least when I was "acting casual" I had something to distract myself from thinking of all the things that could go wrong. I actually ended up filing the crumpled papers properly, just to give myself something productive to do besides worry.

I was so relieved when Dr. Nic arrived that I nearly ran to him with open arms.

Without pausing to greet me, he shoved a bundle of cloth into my hands. "These are the dials and switches on the tank control panels you need to change, and the numbers you need to change them to," he gushed, evidently out of breath.

I untangled the cloth and held it up. It was a shirt of Nic's—a dirty one at that. I wrinkled my nose and glanced up at him.

He shrugged. "Tower had a marker but no paper."

I turned the shirt around to find a mess of numbers and diagrams scribbled on the back in permanent marker.

"This is a diagram of the control panels on the side of the holding tanks. If you flip these switches, it will drain all the product from the factory into the two main holding tanks and seal them off." He gestured at some of the markings on the shirt, then pointed out across the factory to where the two huge tanks extended up the wall.

"Then if you move these dials to the right numbers, it will begin to chill the gas to the point of condensing. Then all we have to do is puncture the bottom of the holding tanks, and the liquid acid will drain safely out the bottom."

I wasn't sure there was a truly "safe" way to drain lethal acid, but, glancing across the factory, I saw what he meant. If we punctured the bottom of the holding tanks while the acid was in liquid form, it would drain down into the factory below, where it would destroy the unwanted equipment and—hopefully—nothing else.

I nodded. "Got it."

"Wait until I give the signal. I have to shut down production first, and then the tanks have to fill completely before we can close them off and condense the gas. Don't touch anything until I tell you to." He turned and ran for the control room without waiting for confirmation.

I headed towards the holding tanks—then remembered they could only be accessed by the narrow catwalk that extended over the machinery. Shuddering, I stared straight ahead and charged across the catwalk as fast as I could force myself, trying to ignore the groan of the working machinery below me.

With another shiver, I ducked onto the platform where the control access was mounted. The massive motors on the side of the tanks extended over the controls, forming a rather cramped alcove. As I squatted on the platform, I understood why Commander Ambrose had assigned Dr. Nic to work here—it must have been torture for someone as tall as Nic to work in so narrow a space for hours on end.

I spread the shirt on the ground and studied it, trying to find the appropriate switches and dials. Dr. Nic's rushed handwriting took some work to decipher, but I found all the right routing switches. The first step was to adjust a dial so that the product from the factory would flow into the tank at full speed.

I laid my hand on the dial, waiting for the signal. I rehearsed the steps in my head. Tank it, condense it, then puncture the tanks and…

I stopped, the full implications of our plan hitting me. Puncture the tanks? We were about to puncture two-story-high tanks filled with a shipload of dangerous chemicals—with the intent of flooding the entire factory with enough acid to melt it into the ground.

That was an extremely violent act of rebellion if there ever was one.

My father's last instructions echoed through my head. *Just do as they say. Go with them quietly and they'll go easier on you.*

Go quietly.

No one has to die. You can stay and not have to work on Red Rain. All you have to do is be quiet for a few hours while I clean up your mess, and then it will be done.

I closed my eyes, remembering those words. Remembering the screech of the security panel denying access. Remembering the crash of metal and glass tubes on the floor. Remembering the explosion. Remembering the voice that cursed me.

And now that same voice shouted at me. "Now, Phil!"

I cranked the first dial for all I was worth.

17

I sat back on my haunches and surveyed the flashing control panel. As near as I could figure, I had rerouted the flow of chemicals correctly. Now I had to wait for the tanks to fill before I could seal them off and start condensing the gas. I had a pretty good guess which display would tell me when the tanks were full, but Dr. Nic had said he would give the signal. For lack of anything else to do to speed the process along, I watched the numbers on the display climb.

They climbed steadily at first, then suddenly jumped. I watched with slightly worried amusement as the numbers on the display spun in a nearly indistinguishable blur.

Abruptly, the display froze. The ominous number 99999—completely maxed out—filled every slot on the display board.

I chewed my lip. Did that mean the tanks were full? Was it time?

I became aware of a high-pitched whirring coming from the factory equipment below me. I crawled to the edge of the alcove and glanced towards the control room, looking for a signal from

Dr. Nic. I could just see his bobbing head bent over the computers.

The whirring grew louder, enough to make my ears tingle. I summoned the courage to look over the edge of the platform at the tangled mess of pipes and tanks below.

Nothing seemed amiss, but I could hear the moan and grumble of machines laboring heavily. Hadn't Dr. Nic shut down production? Shouldn't the machines be quiet? I sensed a slight tremble through the floor; was that normal?

Before I could decide, one of the pipes below me cracked and split open.

I shrieked and threw myself to the floor. I heard more metal breaking and clattering to the ground. I curled into a ball and shielded myself, expecting lethal acid to spray everywhere, but suddenly there was silence.

I cautiously sat up and looked over the edge. The network of pipes was split in multiple places, but nothing poured out of the broken ends. After a moment of listening carefully, I detected the soft hiss of air escaping from somewhere.

And then I remembered. Red Rain was still in gas form. A gas that was now leaking out all over the factory.

I forced myself to breathe normally. I hated to think I was inhaling the stuff, but I knew it couldn't hurt me… right? Could it condense inside me? Could it burn me from the inside out?

I struggled to slow my heart rate, but Dr. Nic's panicked shout sent it racing again.

"Phil, get out of there!"

I turned towards the control room. He had stepped out of the door and was leaning over the railing, waving his arms at me. "The entire system is failing!"

I stood up, my heart flooding with despair. It was my fault; I must have set the dials wrong—

Dr. Nic unwittingly assuaged my guilt. "The virus sent the system into overdrive. You need to get out of there! It thinks the factory is on fire and it's going to—"

He was drowned out by the sudden wail of sirens.

Warning lights started flashing from every direction. And then the emergency sprinklers turned on.

Miraculously, I had the presence of mind to dive backwards as water showered over the factory. With an almost indistinguishable hiss, it met the gases in the air and instantly turned into bright orange-red acid.

I screamed and put my hands over my face, bracing myself for the burns. It took me several seconds to realize nothing was happening. Looking up, I realized the tank motors over the alcove shielded me from the shower.

Pressing myself flat against the tanks, I looked out across the factory. Red Rain showered over the catwalk, cutting off my escape. There was no way for me to reach the exit without entering the downpour.

The exit! There was an emergency panel by the elevator door; the sprinklers could be shut off from there. Dr. Nic could reach the door; the control room and the path to the exit were out of the range of the sprinklers.

Dr. Nic was still shouting at me. Disregarding whatever he was saying, I leaned forward as far as I dared and yelled back, "The emergency panel by the door! Shut off the sprinklers!"

Thankfully he could hear me over the sirens. He glanced towards the exit. I shouted again for emphasis. "Shut them off! Hurry!"

"Just hang on!" he shouted back. "I need to grab the drive! Don't move!"

He darted back into the control room before I could protest. I tried not to feel insulted. He was leaving me here, surrounded by a shower of scalding chemicals, while he went back for the flash drive? What did he even need the drive for? We had uploaded the virus; our job was done.

Then I remembered what else was on the flash drive. The original files for Red Rain. Dr. Nic's copy, which presumably hadn't been affected by the virus.

The realization made my head spin with anger and betrayal. I wanted to scream, but I didn't know what to say. I was crushed by the overwhelming feeling that I had failed. All this meant nothing if Dr. Nic still had a copy of the research.

He had tricked me. I told myself I shouldn't be surprised, but that wasn't true. I was surprised. I had believed him; I had trusted him. And that made it hurt all the worse.

Unable to go anywhere, I clutched my knees to my chest and rocked from side to side, struggling between equally vicious urges to seethe and cry.

The sound of metal crashing nearby startled me out of my thoughts. I turned to see a gaping hole in the catwalk. An entire section was missing from the middle.

It took me a moment to process what was happening. Red Rain was eating away at the metal. Even as I watched, a weakened seam snapped, sending another piece of the catwalk tumbling down to the factory below.

Now I really was trapped.

Despair briefly flooded me, but I fought it back with prayer and common sense. There *had* to be another way off this platform. Surely they had built a second access to the control panel in case of emergency.

I got to my knees and looked around the alcove. There, sandwiched in the narrow space between the tank motors, was a service ladder that led upwards.

I crawled forward and traced the ladder's path. It went up the wall between the tanks, just barely out of reach of the sprinklers. I couldn't see what was above the tanks, but it was my only option.

I stood up, wedged myself between the motors, and struggled to hoist myself onto the ladder. Ironically, it probably would have been easier for someone taller than me, but I managed to get my feet onto the first rung by pushing off of the control panel.

I paused to take a deep breath and adjust my grip. Then I started climbing. It was more strenuous than I imagined, but I focused on finding a steady rhythm. One hand, one foot, next hand, next foot, always testing my grip. I kept breathing deeply in between moves, trying to ignore the sound of the self-destructing factory below me.

As I neared the top, I saw that pipes extended out of the top of the tanks and ran along the ceiling. Presumably that was how they transferred the product from the factory to the ship for transport. Another narrow service catwalk, hanging by steel chains from the ceiling, followed the pipes. It hung just above the network of emergency sprinklers, making it safely out of reach of the hazardous shower.

Praising God, I carefully climbed off the ladder onto the catwalk. The pathway bounced and swayed under my weight. I shrieked and dropped to my knees, causing the catwalk to swing all the more. Swallowing a sudden onset of nausea, I closed my eyes and waited for the movement to subside. *Just go slowly. It will be all right.*

I didn't have the guts to try and stand, so I crawled, trying to make as little motion as possible. The catwalk still bounced, making my stomach and heart bounce with it, but I kept moving forward steadily. I could see a ladder at the other end—my escape to safety.

After getting halfway across the factory, I made the mistake of glancing down. The pipes for the sprinklers were affixed to the underside of the catwalk, and I could see the showers of acid rain right below me. I could have reached out and touched the lethal liquid.

The thought made me shudder, so I quickly looked back up and focused my eyes on the ladder ahead.

The sirens and lights still continued full blast, but I had already begun to tune out the monotony. In the self-imposed silence, I perceived the sound of something gurgling through the pipes above my head. I looked up and saw that there were boxes spaced periodically along the pipeline. The boxes were wet with condensation, and I heard the faint sound of fans whirring.

Cooling containers. They must be shipping the product in liquid form; while dangerous, it would be far more space efficient. These pipes must condense the gas as it flowed up to the shipping yard on the surface. That was why the cooling containers had condensation on them.

No sooner had I processed the thought than I realized the condensation was also turning into acid and eating away at the exterior of the containers. And I knew full well that the exterior was not formulated to resist corrosion.

I saw it coming and had time to scramble backwards before a crack split in the cooling container above my head. A stream of Red Rain gushed out and poured over the catwalk in front of me. It was a narrow stream, but it was enough to block the way. I could only watch in despair as the acid ate away at my last chance of escape.

The metal of the catwalk was thin, and it took only moments before the acid had eaten completely through it—and the chains supporting it. Before I had time to react, the chains snapped, and the section of catwalk dropped from beneath my feet.

I screamed and scrabbled for any handhold, managing to grab another chain. For a perilous moment, I dangled by one hand over the imploding factory. The broken sprinkler line beneath me continued to spray water from both ends, sending Red Rain flying in all directions. A few drops grazed my leg.

I wanted to scream as the tiny burns peppered my skin, but I didn't have enough breath. The world spun and blurred, and I could hardly grasp what was happening. *Oh, God, help!* was the only thought I could gasp out.

He answered by giving me the strength to reach my other hand up and grasp the chain. Even though my body was writhing in pain, I managed to haul myself back onto the catwalk. The remaining sections swayed wildly, but their chains were still intact—for now.

Clarity rushed to my head as I was able to process the situation. I couldn't reach the ladder to the exit. The other ladder only led back to the control platform, where the catwalk was also washed out. There was nowhere to run, and it was only a matter of time before Red Rain corroded the other chains and sent me plummeting into the remains of the factory below, where the acid was rapidly pooling.

I was going to die.

My heart buckled in surrender. I gasped for breath, my mind spinning out of control. Reality slipped from my grasp. The world washed out around me, my head too dizzy to focus. My ears rang with a strange sound—a subtle, rhythmic beep. It was much more calming than the hissing and crackling of Red Rain as it devoured metal, so I focused on it. I closed my eyes and concentrated on it, trying to identify it.

And then I remembered. The beeping of electrical equipment. The sterile scent of sheets. The austere white lighting in the medical bay. And my brother's worried tone.

You were pushing it, though. That close to the explosion, had you not been near an outside wall...

My own voice answered him. *It would have been worth it.*

I took a deep breath. The repulsive scent of Red Rain and corroded metal filled my nostrils, but I didn't fear it. I opened my eyes and looked down at the red sea below me.

"It was worth it."

18

Somewhere across the factory, another chain snapped. I closed my eyes, choosing not to look at the ones closest to me. I didn't want to watch the acid drip and tick off the countdown to my own death.

The factory continued to scream in agony below. Machines hissed and ground as metal cracked and split. The sirens continued unabated, just in case anyone was questioning the ongoing state of emergency.

Despite the din, I was still startled when a human voice yelled at me. "Philadelphia!"

I looked down. Far below, Nic was inching along the outer wall, trying to stay out of the spray as he made his way towards the door.

I sat up. I could think of many colorful words I wanted to shout at him—most of which he had probably inadvertently taught me. None of them seemed sufficient to convey the anger I was suddenly feeling towards him. I settled for the woefully inadequate, "You idiot!"

If he heard me, he accepted the accusation without objection. "I'm coming!"

"Ten minutes too late!" I screeched.

This time, he simply ignored me.

I pinched my eyes shut. It was hopeless; both of the walkways were washed out. What was he going to do?

Suddenly, with a deep-throated purr echoing from somewhere beyond the walls, the factory grew strangely silent. I opened my eyes to see Dr. Nic cranking the levers on the emergency panels. He shut the sprinklers off, followed by most of the power. The water dried, taking the sound of sizzling acid with it. The factory shuddered to a halt and groaned in relief as the machines ceased their endless whirring.

I let out my frustrations in a salty breath. Words could—and would—be exchanged later. But if it was a choice between taking my anger to the grave and accepting an improbable rescue from my unlikely ally, I would swallow my emotions in favor of hoping we might actually make it out of here alive.

Nic walked to the edge of the platform and surveyed the damage. About a third of the catwalk remained on his end— almost enough to reach beneath me, but not quite.

Nic looked down. I followed his gaze to the puddles of Red Rain shimmering on the factory floor. They were bubbling and gurgling but gradually receding as they melted through the concrete floor and soaked into the rocky dirt below.

"Just hang on!" he shouted unhelpfully. "As soon as a path clears, we'll get you down!"

It wasn't a bad plan, but that didn't stop the anger from nipping at my consciousness. I took deep breaths, coaching myself internally. As long as my perch held, everything would be fine.

As if objecting to my optimism, another chain snapped.

I looked around wildly before remembering that sudden motions caused the catwalk to sway. I clung to the chain in panic, then regretted my actions as I felt the chain loosen and start to give way.

Despite the shuddering of the catwalk, I had the sense to let go of the chain and push myself backwards into the middle of the pathway. The chain held, but it was little consolation. I watched in abject horror as a trail of Red Rain dripped from a now-silent fan and dribbled down one of the few remaining chains supporting my section of catwalk.

It was clear from the groaning and shuddering of the other chains that they wouldn't support my weight once one of them snapped.

"Did you hear me, Phil?" Nic called.

"I don't think we have time to wait!" I shrieked. "These chains aren't going to hold!"

For once, Nic seemed to take my concerns seriously. Even from this distance, I could see the panic coloring his face.

Before he could offer any helpful suggestions, another voice joined the chaos. "What have you done?"

The door slammed open—or, I imagine Commander Ambrose would have slammed the doors open had they not been elevator doors. To his credit, he at least had the respect to pause and survey our work before saying anything more.

"What did you expect? You left *her* alone unsupervised," Dr. Nic chirped. I couldn't tell if his sarcasm was genuine or an attempt to deflect Ambrose's rage.

In either case, his humor didn't land. With a warning snarl, Ambrose lunged at Nic, throwing him backwards into the already weakened railing. Nic's lanky frame nearly flipped right over the edge. He hardly had time to find his footing before Ambrose threw a solid punch in his face.

"Don't!" I screamed. I could tell by the look in Ambrose's eyes that this fight was going to end quickly. I had seen him grow lethal on the ship—and there was no one to stop him now.

Dr. Nic dodged the next punch but couldn't avoid the kick that swiftly followed. With a groan even I could hear, he buckled over and retreated three steps. Ambrose charged at him shoulder-first like a bull. Nic sidestepped into the only space available—the catwalk.

Realizing he'd cornered his prey, Ambrose grinned and slowed his approach. "I hope you enjoyed your little act of rebellion," he sneered. He advanced and forced Nic to back down the narrow walkway.

For once, Nic didn't answer.

"Because once you're out of the picture," Ambrose jabbed Nic's shoulder, "we'll just rebuild and pick up right where we left off."

"I know you will," Nic coughed, "after you finish repairing all the damage from the virus I just released on your perfect little United internet."

Ambrose cocked his head in confusion. Nic took a deep breath and straightened to his full height. "You really do have a great upload speed, especially for being so far out in the ocean."

I caught myself smiling with pride—a feeling that evaporated when Ambrose howled. With the speed of a viper, he backhanded Nic.

I squealed. "Please, stop!"

Nic slid three more steps backwards—to the end of the catwalk. He twisted around, scanning the wreckage of the factory below him.

I realized that he could make the jump—if there weren't puddles of acid everywhere.

The commander closed the gap. I sat up on my knees, straining to be heard. "Ambrose! Please, don't do this!"

He hesitated long enough to cast a venomous look in my direction. "Don't think you aren't next, darling."

And then he lunged at Nic.

I screamed—and then nearly choked on the sound as my heart leapt to my throat. With the agility of a lynx, Nic ducked. Ambrose, too slow and heavy to stop his forward motion, tumbled over him. Nic swiped at his legs and easily set him flying over the edge.

Ambrose didn't even have time to yell before he landed—face-first in a puddle of Red Rain.

I wanted to scream again—but at that moment, a chain snapped.

The catwalk plunged backwards as the far corner gave away. Thrown to my hands and knees, I scrabbled at the platform, my palms tearing and bleeding on the rough metal, searching for a handhold.

"Nic!" I squeaked out.

If he answered me, I couldn't hear him. Like violin strings taunting my demise, the other three chains quivered and groaned. Then without further ado, the chain behind me broke. The platform swung down like a trapdoor, gracelessly hurling me into the factory below.

I plummeted backwards towards the ground. I lost all breath to cry out as the wind rushed around me like waves cocooning a drowning ship. Eerily suspended in air, my voice gone and my vision blurred, I hung in a moment of unearthly silence as my last thought crystalized.

Goodbye, Daddy.

And then I hit the ground.

At first, my landing seemed strangely soft—and then my neck snapped backwards and hit hard concrete, finally sending me into permanent darkness.

19

I could hear long before I could see. Noises murmured in my mind, murky and unclear like they came through water. For a while, I felt like I was floating, unable to feel anything except for the vague sense of motion around me.

My consciousness pushed back against the waves. *Let me out!*

The darkness slowly melted into light—blinding, burning light. My sense of smell returned, bringing with it the taste of salt, ash, and blood. I was grateful—because without the sulfuric stench, I probably would have thought I was dead.

As it was, I was still a little disappointed when the world came into focus and the first person I saw was Dr. Nic.

A voice somewhere behind me murmured, "She'll be all right."

And then, like a puzzle snapping together, consciousness rushed at me. The first thing I became aware of was the *grinding* headache I had. Then I saw the noonday sky above me, punctured by the misshapen buildings of Rott. I heard guards barking orders, a distant siren, and the sea slapping against the shore like it didn't care.

I managed to push past the pain to formulate a clear thought. *You made it. You're alive.*

Thank you, Jesus.

I put out my palms and felt beneath me. I was lying on a rough medical cot of some kind. Gripping the sides with as much strength as I could muster, I started to rise.

Nic's palm met my shoulder and shoved me back. "Don't you *dare.*"

His voice cracked. Startled, I squinted and focused on his face. He was glaring at me so intently that at first I thought he must be angry. His expression was so strange, almost disconcerting in a way—not because it was hard to read, but because I had never seen him look that way at anyone, much less me, before.

He looked worried. And then, maybe just a little bit relieved.

I smiled.

Tower disrupted the moment by stepping into my line of vision. "Sounds like you two had fun down there." He squatted next to my cot.

No longer distracted by sentimentality, I was again accosted by the magnitude of my headache. "Yeah, and I have the hangover to prove it." I paused, acknowledging the gaps in my memory. "What happened?"

Tower's unkempt eyebrows shot up, almost disappearing into his shaggy bangs. "I was hoping you would fill in the details. What exactly did you do to the computers?"

"Wasn't that a gem?" Nic inserted, still sounding a bit salty about the virus. "*I* came up with the original concept for that—"

"No," I interrupted. The pain was making it very difficult to string thoughts together, and I was losing patience. "I mean, how did I survive? I fell. I remember hitting the ground." I blinked, for the first time appreciating the miracle. *How am I still alive?*

Tower deferred to Nic with a sideways glance. I followed his gaze. "Nic, did you..."

He avoided my eyes. "Something broke your fall."

"Mostly," Tower added. "You did get a nasty concussion."

"We are going to need to get you checked out," Nic agreed. "That's your second head injury in a week."

I grunted, frustrated. What did any of that matter? "Fine, whatever. But how did you—"

"It doesn't matter."

"But Nic—"

He cut me off with another harsh glare. This time, he was clearly angry. "When are you going to learn that not all unanswered questions are bad omens? Sometimes it's okay to leave a door shut."

I opened my mouth, grappling for a protest, but found none. Even though I didn't know why, I decided to take his advice—just this once.

Diffusing the tension with a sigh, Tower said, "So, about the computers…"

"Did it work?" I exclaimed, a little too excitedly. I winced as my skull throbbed.

"If you mean every computer on the island is loading a blue screen of death, then yes, it worked."

My heart warmed. *Good job, brother. I hope Cea is proud.*

I flinched as I remembered one missing detail. "What about… Ambrose?"

This time, even Tower refused to look at me. "I'm pretty sure the fall killed him first," Nic said, as if that was any consolation. I shuddered and tried to offer up a prayer, but could come up with no words.

All around us, the din of military orders and general chaos continued. I became aware of a familiar voice approaching out of the crowd and turned to see the captain striding towards us, flanked by at least six other heavily armed officers.

Tower hastily stood up. "Well, you two are going to jail for a very long time."

"Thank God," Nic muttered—and, surprisingly, he didn't sound sarcastic about it.

With another nod at me, Tower melded into the crowd.

The captain stopped next to me and leaned over, blocking out the sky with his imposing shadow. "I'm impressed," he said in a tone as dry as sand. "You're the first convicted 'terrorist' the United has sent me that has actually managed to perpetrate an act of terrorism."

I cringed. "Thanks?"

Dr. Nic stood up, matching the captain in height. "What, did our reputation not precede us?"

The captain ignored the comment. "Care to explain to me why my computers seemed to have been wiped of their data, young man?"

Nic nodded smartly. "It would be my pleasure."

The captain flicked his head, and two of the guards flanked Nic and handcuffed him. He seemed entirely unbothered by it all.

The captain looked down at me. "Take her to the infirmary, and put her under guard. I don't want any more incidents until they're shipped back to the mainland for trial."

"Trial?" I gasped.

The captain eyed me condescendingly. "I only deal with convicted criminals. Since you two have taken it upon yourselves to commit a new crime, you'll have to answer to the United for that."

My head spun, although whether from confusion or the developing brain injury, it was hard to tell. Of course our little stunt wouldn't go unnoticed. The United was going to want all the details about the virus we had unleashed—and then what? Would they kill us? Send us back to prison? Would this affect Ephesus? Cea? My father? Where were they?

I pinched my eyes shut, partially to quell the pain and partially to hide the tears that spontaneously formed.

"Hey." The gentle reprimand tapped my ear. I looked up to find Dr. Nic gazing at me again. "It will be all right."

Before he could elaborate on that sentiment, the guards prodded his shoulder and pushed him across the yard. Dr. Nic went without resistance or another glance at me.

My skull was throbbing so much that I hardly noticed when two of the other guards lifted my cot and started carrying me across the yard. I covered my face with my hands to block out the harsh sun, focusing instead on taking slow breaths.

I wasn't quite ready to trust Dr. Nic with much of anything. But I supposed, given the circumstances, I could follow his lead and let things go for a few hours.

Besides, I knew he was right, even if for different reasons. Come what may, things would work out for good.

20

I underestimated the United's eagerness to interrogate us. I was only in the infirmary for a few hours, doted on by a nurse who seemed more interested in pressing me for all the gossipy details about our crime than he was in examining my injuries, before a helicopter arrived to ferry us back to the mainland.

Deemed "fit to travel" by the useless nurse, I was handcuffed and crammed onto the stuffy helicopter with a chained Nic and several armed guards. Nic seemed in good spirits and cast several grins in my direction. I decided it was not a good idea to risk conversation while my forearm was pressed against a holstered gun, so I didn't ask him what he was so stupidly happy about.

Despite the unease in the air, I was nevertheless comforted by the sight of the mainland bleeding into the horizon. I had no idea if this was the same port we had taken off from, and I didn't recognize any of the geography, so we could have been halfway down the coast for all I knew. But it didn't matter—it was still one step closer to my family.

If I was honest with myself, I didn't have any hope that our escapades would inspire the government to reunite us. If anything, they probably realized I was a danger regardless of where I was imprisoned, and solitary confinement and maximum security were likely in my future, if they even kept me alive.

But for some reason, the prospect didn't bother me. I had no idea where my family was or what had been done with them. But as the helicopter lowered itself onto the green earth, I reminded myself: My family was on this soil, somewhere. And that was enough for now.

Our new ride was a train, of all things—and an old one at that. Its metal cars were washed-out shades of green and orange, and its squeaking wheels were so rusted they looked like they might be fused to the tracks. We were hustled to a car at the rear and roughly loaded in like cattle. One guard accompanied us. The door was dragged shut with a screech that plunged my headache to a new level of pain.

A single battery-powered lantern illuminated the dusty interior. They hadn't even bothered to clean out the abandoned crates and dusty tarps left over from the car's shipping days.

The rest of our escort wandered away, their shouts fading from outside the train. Figuring our sole escort wouldn't be too bothered by conversation, I ventured, "Where did they find this old piece of junk?"

Nic shrugged.

"Most of the electric trains aren't working. Something about the navigation system being screwy," the guard offered. I shared an excited glance with Nic. *So the virus did make it back to the mainland.* I shivered with the realization.

If the guard understood the implications, he didn't belay any interest. With a callous pop of his bubble gum, he tossed a pair of keys over his shoulder and walked away. "It'll be a bumpy ride—might want to find something to hang on to." He wandered over to the corner and began amusing himself with a pocket knife.

"Thanks," Nic said. He knelt and fetched the keys from the floor, then gestured at me.

I dumbly held my hands out. "What's going on...?" I said in a half-whisper, wondering if I should have already picked up on the hints.

My handcuffs dropped to the floor. I hastily freed Nic as he explained, "This train is about to get hijacked in..."

"Thirty minutes," the guard offered.

Nic nodded.

"Again?" I exclaimed, the weight of his words hitting me.

"It worked last time, didn't it?"

I had no answer for that. "But how did you—"

"As much as I don't want to admit it, I owe John and Dowe more than a few favors—starting with a new laptop, for some reason."

I squinted. I knew I had underestimated those two, apparently in more ways than one.

"And where will we go after we get 'hijacked'?"

"Depends on who's nearby," Nic replied, seemingly unconcerned with the uncertainty of it all. "But our first step will be to get new prints taken."

"New prints?"

Dr. Nic stretched, popping the joints in his neck. "The most important thing the virus did was screw up databases—including databases of criminal files. They no doubt have offline backups of much of the information, but it will take time to get that restored. Until then, we have a narrow opportunity where it will be very easy for certain gifted individuals to falsify personnel files."

He looked up at me. "If this goes well, by the time they get the systems back online, our fingerprints will be associated with new names and new files."

A new name? But what will I call myself? How will I find my family if they also wipe their files and change their names? My broken mind struggled to jump through the hoops, but it kept tripping over one seemingly obvious roadblock.

"You mean... they can get the systems back online?"

"Eventually. What can't be restored will be replaced."

"But the virus…"

"Nothing is perfect. I'm confident we wreaked havoc in their top-level systems, because that computer on Rott was connected to one of their major government servers. It was their big project of the year, and that will be their downfall. But there will always be alternate connections, private servers, and good firewalls. They didn't lose everything—but they have much bigger problems to solve than some missing criminal files."

"But that means…" I couldn't formulate the words, partially because my head hurt and partially because I didn't want to say them out loud for fear they might be true. "They might still have Red Rain."

Nic didn't say anything at first, which was just as well. The train's engine roared to life, sending a rumble reverberating through the cars. The noise grew louder and louder, punctuated by several sharp screeches of the whistle. Despite having several minutes of warning, it still startled me when the train jerked forward, sending me sprawling on the floor.

"I told you to find a handhold," the guard admonished.

Pulling myself to a seating position, I found a handle near the door and stabilized myself against the wall. I watched the shifting light seeping through the cracks in the boards as we pulled out of the station, the train picking up speed with slow determination. Eventually, it seemed to find its rhythm, and despite the grinding of the wheels and the soft shake of the car back and forth, the noise became bearable.

I looked to Dr. Nic, expecting an answer.

He met my gaze boldly. "It's possible."

My heart shattered, although I somehow managed to avoid crying out with the anguish I felt.

"But that's why you need this."

He drew his hand from his pocket and held out a slender object. I gasped when I recognized it in the weak light. *My brother's flash drive.*

"But you—" My voice turned accusatory once I remembered what else was on that drive.

"I deleted Red Rain," he assured me. "That's why it took me so long. I know that's not an excuse, but I had to make sure it was gone."

The fact that he continued to hold my gaze told me he was being honest. He was right—it wasn't an excuse. But somehow I didn't have the energy to be mad.

"But the rest of your brother's work should still be on here. It's hard to know, because that virus is incredibly thorough and deadly, but I think everything is intact."

He pressed it into my open palm. "Keep it. You will need it. If not for Red Rain, then for something else. The rebellion will need weapons. We 'terrorists' lost a lot of work today too—we're going to have to start somewhere."

He paused, as if contemplating his own words. "We may no longer be fighting with chemicals, but we still have to win a war."

I closed my fist around the drive. "Thanks."

By way of reply, he smiled.

The remainder of the ride passed in silence. I was far too consumed with attempting to process my spiraling thoughts—as best I could around my receding headache—to solicit any more conversation.

As promised, in about half an hour the train began to slow. Our guard stood up and walked over to the door. "You might want to stand back," he advised me.

Scrambling backwards to the middle of the car, I watched in horror as the guard callously dragged the door open. With the force of a tornado, heavy wind gushed into the cabin, bringing with it the furious noise of the train laboring across the tracks. I squatted close to the ground, hoping my low profile would prevent me from getting blown away.

The guard leaned precariously out the door and looked around. "There's the drop site—that rooftop around the bend."

"Rooftop?" I screeched, unable to contain my rising panic any longer.

The only consolation I got was another annoying pop of his bubble gum. "Yup. You're going to have to jump, tuck, and roll."

Having—literally—nothing else to hang onto at this point, I looked to Nic in a desperate grab for assurance. He shrugged. "It's a hijacking. The train isn't exactly going to stop and let us off."

I pinched my eyes shut, fighting a premature wave of nausea. *Oh dear Lord, help us.*

"Hey," he urged, "how is this any scarier than blowing up a whole factory of chemicals?"

I glared at him—mainly because I knew he was right.

"Here she comes," the guard warned.

Standing up slowly, I took a brave step towards the door— and stumbled as the train lurched around a bend. With a scream I fell forward and slammed into the broad side of the door. Thankfully it held.

"Be careful," Nic said, sounding a mix of concerned and sarcastic.

Taking deep breaths, I found the door handle and used it to pull myself over to the opening. Muttering prayers, I swallowed and dared to open my eyes.

The world rushed past so quickly it was just a blinding whirl of color. We were on elevated tracks, racing at least two stories above the ground.

Oh God, I can't do this... I forced myself to hold steady, trying to match the rhythm of my breaths with the clacking of the train. *Just one jump, and you can start a new life.*

It took a minute of coaching, but the scenery slowly came back into focus. City buildings began to punctuate the countryside as we rapidly approached a sprawling town.

Nic appeared beside me. "It won't be a far jump. The tracks run right between the buildings. You can do it."

I have to.

Despite his candor, I could tell Dr. Nic was also bracing himself for the leap. "Just try not to hit your head again, okay?" he offered, his joviality cracking somewhat.

I was about to answer when the thought rushed past me, almost as fast and fleeting as the wind grinding against the train.

You should learn to program.

I felt the flash drive shifting in my shoe. Being able to manipulate computers had gotten my father and brother out of trouble and into favored jobs more than once. Dr. Nic had built an entire colony with a carefully-programmed private server. And I had just witnessed the chaos a well-designed computer virus could deal to the United.

The rebellion will need weapons.

Shouts ricocheted off the tracks ahead. The train careened around a curve, and I could see figures swarming on a low, flat-topped building about a half-mile ahead.

"Brace yourself!" Nic hollered, almost a second too late. The brakes kicked in, drowning out all conversation with a high-pitched screech as the train lurched violently.

I gripped the door with both hands. My heart was racing, but, for the first time in several weeks, it wasn't from fear.

We have to start somewhere.

The rooftop loomed closer. I could hear yelling over the scream of the brakes and vaguely understood that Nic was giving me instructions. I stepped back and prepared to run, one last thought solidifying in my mind and filling my legs with courage.

I may not be a scientist. I didn't know how to handle guns, and I definitely didn't want to design weapons of mass destruction.

But I could still fight.

The train leveled in front of the long building. A group of strangers hovered with open arms ready to receive us. Nic shouted at me.

"I'm coming, Daddy," I said aloud.

And then I jumped.

TO BE CONTINUED...

PRISONER 120518

RED RAIN #2.5

RACHEL NEWHOUSE
& DAVID HARTUNG

THERE'S MORE TO THE STORY ...

I made it back to my cell just before the door automatically locked, signaling curfew. I turned out the light, slid the cover across the barred window of the door, and sat down at the desk to wait. I'm not sure why the cell had a desk—I hadn't seen a single book or piece of paper on the entire island—but sitting at the empty desk was slightly less dehumanizing than curling up on the weak cot that was too short for my lanky frame.

It wasn't ten minutes later that I heard heavy footsteps and winded breaths enter the corridor. He stopped outside my cell, blocking out the silver of light that crept in under the door.

"Let's talk," he said by way of introduction.

Let's not. I decided to ignore him, mostly just to see what he'd do.

"120518, I know you're in there."

What a Sherlock.

"Open the window."

Nah. I crossed my leg, leaned back in the chair, and waited.

He grunted and cussed. I heard keys rattle, then a swipe of a card in the door. It rejected him with a beep.

I couldn't resist a laugh into the darkness. They hadn't even given him access privileges.

He heard me and swore again. "Open up!"

"You want me to open the door from the inside? That's not how prisons work."

"Do it or I kill you."

"What kind of threat is that? You can't shoot me through the door, unless they gave you one of the good guns, but I don't think you have the clearance."

He mumbled into his communicator.

I lazily stood up and strolled to the door. "How pathetic. You have me in prison on the mainland for months—months!—and hardly say a word to me. Now you swim across the Atlantic to track me down, and you can't even get the door open."

I slid the cover back from the window, revealing an electric pistol aimed at the bars. I was right—it wouldn't have punctured the steel door. It was a child's weapon, really, perfectly suited to the childish man.

I put my hands up. "Please, go ahead. Shoot me. I've been waiting six months for one of you to have the courage."

He spat at me, but the spittle just landed on the handle of his own gun. He grimaced and wiped his hand on his pants.

"What do you want?" I asked. "It's past my bedtime."

He composed himself and put on a smile. "How are you liking Rott, 'Q'?" he slithered, lines clearly rehearsed.

"Don't even try. If you think I'm going to play that song and dance, you're wrong. Just tell me what you want so I can make a show of pondering your offer before slamming this shut in your face." I kept my hand on the window for emphasis.

"You're no fun. At least the Christians put on a good show."

"Then why don't you go back to supervising them, Ambrose? Go back to your cute little concentration camp with a cushy office and a dozen underlings to do your bidding. Go back to watching a bunch of spineless martyrs who don't have the gumption to scale a six-foot wall. Take the easy paycheck, you deserve it."

He was less bothered by that statement than I expected— probably because it was all true, and he didn't mind admitting it. "Maybe when I retire. Right now, though, I've received a better offer."

"Wonderful. I hope your promotion takes you far away from me."

"That is the only downside to this position—it dictates that you and I will be working very closely for the next few months."

"That tells me everything I need to know—I'm not interested, and goodbye."

I slid the window shut. He gave a startled noise I took some pleasure in.

"If you don't…" He swallowed the threat and reinstated his professionalism. "You haven't even heard the employee benefits yet."

"There's nothing you could offer me that would justify those working conditions."

He chuckled. "Really? There's nothing you want? Nothing at all that I could tempt you with? What *do* you want? Money? A state-of-the-art lab? Your own island?"

"I'd consider my own planet. If you offered me Mars, I'd probably play ball, but anything less than that—not interested."

"Your own planet, huh? I think that can be arranged."

"Oh really."

"Well, maybe not a whole planet but—"

"You're lying? How did I know."

"—I think we could spare a moon."

I walked back to the desk. He kept talking, his voice slightly muffled through the door. "We could set you up on a nice, deserted moon. Give you all the supplies you need to build up your own self-sufficient base. Send a few scientists with you to keep you company. We couldn't give you interstellar travel, of course—you've proven you're not trustworthy with it—but we could abandon you to the stars to be the ruler of your own little kingdom."

I stopped, folded my arms, and waited for him to go away.

"That's what you want, isn't it? To be in control. To be free from government regulations and run your own life. To be alone."

I looked to the ceiling. "That last part is spot-on. Can I go to bed now?"

"I have the power. I know the people. I've been authorized to offer you whatever you want, if you'll just do one little project for me."

"And what project is that? What could I possibly offer you that would be worth such a price?"

He savored the moment a beat too long. "Red Rain," he cooed. "You could give us Red Rain, Dr. Nic."

AVAILABLE NOW!

ANDROMEDA
RED RAIN #3
RACHEL NEWHOUSE

AND IT ISN'T OVER YET...

"Jump, tuck, and roll," they'd said.

It was only after I took a running leap off the moving train that I realized I had no idea how to execute that.

In the split second of panic as I hurled from the train to the building, my muscles did the only thing they could think of. I curled into a ball and threw my hands over my head as the roof rushed up to catch me. My landing was more of a "splay" than a "roll" as I crashed hip-first onto the concrete.

I moaned as the inertia shuddered through my bones. The skin on my right leg screamed, reminding me that the chemical burn I'd sustained this morning was fresh and festering. At least I was wearing thick jeans and long sleeves.

I looked up and was privately gratified to find that my traveling companion hadn't nailed the landing either. Nic stared at his bloody palms and then brushed them off with a wince.

"Can you walk?" he said as he struggled to do the same.

"Yeah." I knew nothing was broken; my hip and thigh would probably just wear a bruise for the next decade. It would go nicely with the leg scars I was no doubt developing under the layers of bandages.

I grasped the ledge and hauled myself up. I glanced over the edge of the roof and nearly vomited. Not because of the height—it was only two stories—but because of the headache that was ramming into my skull like a bull beating down a gate. This was the third time this week that I'd taken a hard impact; it was a wonder I could still remember my name.

I pinched my temples and reminded myself why I had jumped off a moving train. Nic and I had just been deported from the prison island of Rott to be questioned by the United for our various and sundry acts of rebellion—except our train had been "hijacked" by friendly strangers, who, assuming everything was still going to plan, were going to take us to a safe place.

I looked up. Three men were waiting on the roof. They were dressed like maintenance crew, in jackets with a forgettable company logo on the back. If anyone had seen them on the roof prior to our dramatic arrival, I don't think they would have thought anything of it.

I could only hope the passing train had blocked our botched "jump, tuck, and roll" from any nosey passerby.

"Come on," one of the strangers approached me, "we need to get you two out of sight."

He grasped my arm. I was grateful for the guidance; my headache was blurring my sense of direction. He pulled me through the door and down the stairwell to a rear exit, where a windowless white service van was parked in the alley.

Nic followed. "They told me we'd be taking the subway."

"Change of plans." One of them rapped on the rear door of the van. "The subway's been compromised. Our connection didn't make contact. So we're going to have to slog it through rush hour."

The doors opened, and a hand reached out of the shadows in the back of the van. I accepted the offer of help and let the faceless stranger pull me up and guide me into the corner, where I sank down against the wall.

The van rocked as Nic joined us. The doors were slammed and latched without ceremony, plunging us into complete blackness.

"Hang on," an unfamiliar voice said. There was a clatter, and then a weak light flickered on. Our chaperone held a flashlight that cast his features into sharp relief.

I heard the cabin doors shut, and the engine revved to life. The diesel rumble made the whole van shake, and the shudder shot straight up my bones and into my head. I moaned as my headache roared. The whole world swayed, completely out of time with the rocking of the van as it jerked forward. Black spotted my vision.

You're going to pass out. The warning flared across my subconscious. I scooted away from the wall, buried my face in my knees, and closed my eyes. *Breathe. Breathe!* I sucked in a shuddery breath and let it out, then pulled in another. And another.

"Hey. You good?"

Against my better judgment, I lifted my head and looked up. Our escort leaned over me. He'd balanced the flashlight on a nearby crate, projecting its diffused light onto the roof of the van.

"No," I managed, my slurred tone confirming my statement.

"Here, this will help with the nausea." He held out a water bottle—the cap mercifully removed—and a small white pill.

I squinted. "How did you know I was—"

He raised an eyebrow. "You look like death."

I didn't doubt it. I accepted the offerings and gingerly sipped the water. When my stomach didn't refuse it, a took a mouthful and swallowed the pill. Vaguely I wondered where he had gotten it—did they know I had suffered a head injury this morning and came prepared?

Did all that really happen this morning? The day's events flashed through my mind like a movie starring someone else. Nic and I had blown up a factory of dangerous chemicals and released a vicious computer virus onto the internet. We did that. We destroyed the government's superweapon. We crippled the United.

I repeated that fact over and over in my mind, hoping it would ground me in reality. On one hand, our escapades on Rott seemed like a lifetime ago. On the other hand, my body still felt trapped in that self-destructing factory. I heard the endless sirens wailing, smelled the blood-like stench of Red Rain as it burned through the metal machinery and scalded my leg, and felt myself falling, falling...

"Philadelphia." It was Nic this time. He caught me as I swooned. He took the water bottle from my hand and propped me up against a crate. "Deep breaths."

I ignored the admonition; my lungs were fluttering in tune with my heart. "Tell me what happened. Everything."

His eyebrows shot up. "Why?"

"Just do it! I need someone—anyone—to keep talking." I tipped my head back and sucked small breaths in through my nose.

He shifted uncomfortably. "Umm, okay. Where do you want me to start?"

I used my last remaining ounce of motor control to glare at him. I knew our alliance was loose, but he owed me this one. It was his fault I nearly died in that factory today.

"Okay, okay." He sat down cross-legged next to me. "The United captured us—all of us. You, me—"

"Dad. Ephesus." I wrapped my arms around my knees.

"—and Cea. Yes, that's right." He used the same tone you would with a five-year-old; it seemed to help him as much as it was helping me. "They separated us. I don't know where the others are. They sent us to Rott."

"Ambrose," I growled. My anger gave me a moment of mental clarity. "Ambrose is dead."

"Very much so."

I shuddered, remembering his body splattered on the floor of the burning factory. I tried to muster an emotion—any emotion. Commander Ambrose had overseen the unassimilated concentration camp my family had been detained in, until he'd gotten a better offer to help produce Red Rain. He had breathed down my neck for so long—surely his death should rouse some response from me, Christlike or not. Maybe it was the fog in my head, but I felt nothing, and that terrified me.

"Keep talking."

Nic chewed his lip. "They were making Red Rain on Rott."

"Because my dad finished the formula." That was why they'd chased us down and thrown us in prison: to force my father to finish what Nic had started. Presumably they'd threatened to kill me if he didn't, but I'll never know. My father hadn't explained the last time we talked, before they sentenced me to Rott. He hadn't even said goodbye.

Chaotic emotions came at me in a wave, but they were drowned out by a swell of nausea. Whatever that guy had given me, it was *not* helping. I heaved through my nose.

Nic watched me. "Yes, he did. But we destroyed the factory. We set the systems to overload."

"And you uploaded the virus."

"Nasty bugger," our escort inserted himself into the conversation for the first time. He handed Nic another water bottle. "Where in the world did you get a weapon like that?"

I let my muddled mind churn over the question for a minute. "My brother…" Ephesus had made it, along with a bunch of other programs and prototypes—and it was all on a flash drive that was currently wedged in my shoe. I reached for it.

Nic grasped my wrist. "Less talking, more listening." He pushed me back against the crate, then kept talking before I could muster up the cognitive ability to argue. "The United sent us back to the mainland for questioning, but our friends here intercepted us." He nodded at our escort, who gave a sarcastic salute. "We're going to a safe place, where we'll get our files wiped."

"I have to pick a new name," I whispered, remembering.

"That's right." Nic took a swig of his water and grimaced.

I leaned my head against the crate, questions swirling faster than the stars that were dancing in my vision. I knew it was necessary to avoid prosecution—but how? How could I pick a new name? Not only did I have absolutely *no* idea what I'd call myself, but I couldn't imagine being anyone but Philadelphia Smyrna.

Changing my name seemed like the final betrayal, the last shred of my self-autonomy being ripped from my grasp. Despite all the trauma that had happened to me over the past six years—being labeled a criminal and contained in a camp, having my family torn apart multiple times—my name had stayed with me. I was Philadelphia, and that was something not even the government could take from me.

If I'm not Philadelphia, who am I?

I wanted to cry, but the need to vomit was greater. Before I could register what was happening, I wretched.

"Phil!" Nic dropped his water bottle.

"Everything hurts," I moaned, and I meant it. The feeling of pain in every joint of my body was overwhelming—and so *heavy*. I suddenly felt like I'd left Earth's gravity and was slogging through wet concrete.

"What did you do?" Nic yelled, but the question wasn't directed at me. He grabbed his now-empty water bottle and sniffed it. His voice jumped an octave. *"What did you do?"*

Black again splattered my vision, and this time it wouldn't blink away. I couldn't even see the ground as I plunged.

Someone caught me, but I wasn't sure who. They must have laid me down on the ground, because my body stopped moving, but I couldn't feel anything. Not the van floor shuddering beneath me, not the pain in my joints—nothing. For a brief moment, it was almost peaceful.

The last thing I registered before succumbing to the darkness was Nic screeching.

AVAILABLE NOW!

WANT EXCLUSIVE BONUS SCENES?

Become a Patron and get access to **exclusive bonus scenes** for this series! This bonus content is not available anywhere else, and I post a new scene every month. Plus, you can get digital ARCs, signed paperbacks, collector's edition hardbacks, and merch, or read my WIP as I write it!

Become a Patron at:
patreon.com/rachelnewhouse

Or sign up for my newsletter and be the first to hear about new releases—plus get sneak peeks of upcoming books, cover art, and more!

Sign up at:
rachelnewhouse.com/subscribe

DID YOU LOVE THIS BOOK?

Please consider leaving a review on Amazon or Goodreads! It's one of the most important things you can do to support an indie author. Thank you!

SPECIAL THANKS

All the credit (and blame) for this book goes to David J. Hartung, one of my best and loudest fans. Most writers dream of the day when their characters are so famous that others are inspired to write fanfiction about them; I can say I've had that humbling honor early in my career. Whatever possessed David to write an incredibly detailed (and gratifyingly long) fanfiction about the escapades of Dr. Nic I'll never know, but his work was just so ludicrously brilliant that it would have been a crime had I not made it canon. Although my writing cannot hold a candle to the witty sarcasm you brought to the character of Dr. Nic, I hope you're pleased about this monstrosity that you've inspired, David. Always keep writing. You know how I feel about that one story with the troll.

HI FROM RACHEL

Rachel Newhouse is an author, wife, secretary, and Sunday school teacher from Kansas City, Missouri. Her obsessions are sci-fi, dystopian, and kid lit. When she's not writing, she's cooking Asian food, growing chilis that are too spicy to eat, and watching wildly age-inappropriate shows like *My Little Pony* and *Gravity Falls* with her husband, Joe. She also really likes glitter. You've been warned.

Connect with Rachel:
bio.site/rachelnewhouse